"In this fine and deeply moving novel, Timothy O'Grady resists nostalgia ... [it reads with] all the humour and intensity of a real life honestly recorded, and with the pathos mutability lends the past"   LUCY HUGHES-HALLETT, *Sunday Times*

"The direct symbolism of Steve Pyke's stunning photographs matches O'Grady's text beautifully"   MARY LOUDON, *The Times*

"If the words tell the story of the voiceless, the bleak, lovely photographs that accompany it show their faces ... Fiction rarely gets as close to the messy, glorious truth as do memories and photographs. This rare novel dares to use both"
CHARLOTTE MENDELSON, *Times Literary Supplement*

"There is a power and beauty about this novel"
DAVID HORSPOOL, *Daily Telegraph*

"Richly atmospheric, the vivid and lyrical text and starkly beautiful black-and-white photographs bring feelings and images together like the act of memory itself"   *Irish Post*

"This isn't just another Irish exploration of exile but a little masterpiece in which O'Grady has gathered true experiences, then meshed them into one delicate narration"
ANNE SIMPSON, *Glasgow Herald*

"The text is both minimal and musical, in a way that echoes Beckett"   COLE MORETON, *Independent on Sunday*

"There are not many books this year that seem to me written with comparable force, depth of feeling and sardonic pride"
DAN JACOBSON, *Sunday Telegraph*

"What Pyke and O'Grady have done is read our imagination"
DERMOT HEALY

TIMOTHY O'GRADY is the author of the prize-winning novel *Motherland* and co-author with Kenneth Griffith of *Curious Journey: An Oral History of Ireland's Unfinished Revolution* (Mercier Press, Ireland). He was awarded the Encore Award for the best second novel of 1997 for *I Could Read the Sky*.

STEVE PYKE'S photographic books include *Philosophers* and *Poguetry*. His work and installations are exhibited worldwide.

"Everything was the stories my father told me about his life . . . it was as if he was in the room with me again . . . You have put down that feeling of terrible longing that I didn't think anyone but me remembered"

EILEEN GALLAGHER, *in a letter to the author*

Timothy O'Grady
Steve Pyke

I COULD READ
THE SKY

With a preface by John Berger

THE HARVILL PRESS
LONDON

I whispered: memory hurts wherever you touch it.
George Seferis

In remembrance is the secret of redemption.
Holocaust memorial, San Francisco

First published in 1997 by The Harvill Press

www.harvill-press.com

This paperback edition first published in 1998
by The Harvill Press, 2 Aztec Row, Berners Road, London N1 0PW

1 3 5 7 9 8 6 4 2

Text copyright © Timothy O'Grady, 1997
Photographs copyright © Steve Pyke, 1997
Preface copyright © John Berger, 1997

The authors have asserted their moral right

This book is published with the assistance of the Arts Council of England

Timothy O'Grady acknowledges with gratitude his award from
the National Endowment for the Arts, Washington DC

Timothy O'Grady and Steve Pyke acknowledge with gratitude
the financial assistance of the Cultural Relations Committee of
the Irish Department of Foreign Affairs

Sections of this book first appeared in *Force Ten*

None of the photographs in this book are intended to
represent any of its fictional characters

A CIP catalogue record for this book is available from the British Library

ISBN 1 86046 508 0

Designed and typeset in Adobe Caslon
at Libanus Press, Marlborough, Wiltshire

Printed and bound in Great Britain by Mackays of Chatham

Preface

I dare not go deeply into this book, for if I did, I would stay with it forever and I wouldn't return. And then I wouldn't be on this page, as I am now, on this page before the book begins.

Is this a book? A stupid question if ever there was one. What else am I writing a preface to? It's a bastard. It has been made in the dark, as photos are made in a darkroom. It is to be looked at with the eyes shut, not the first time of course, but at all other times when you turn its pages.

Sure, every book, like every blackbird, is different. And sure, when you read here, you hear a chorus behind the talking voice, O'Sullivan and Behan, O'Casey and Synge, Joyce and Jack Yeats (with the hooves of the horses drumming), Beckett and O'Flaherty, they are all here in the dark, protecting with their art the new voice, saving it from oblivion, just as they kept it company when it was alone and wandering.

So what kind of bastard is it?

Every joker knows that making them laugh depends upon timing. It's much easier to make them cry, for sadness accumulates, whereas laughter comes with surprise. Always with surprise. Maybe in the next world it's happily the other way round.

Timing is the skill of playing with silence, of distributing it cunningly, of hiding it so that the listener comes upon it with surprise and delight – like the Russians hide painted eggs at Easter for the children to find. And in a story what is it that silence means? The unsaid, no?

You find the unsaid all the while here. At the top of the page before the lines begin. At the bottom when they're over. And between the lines, between the sentences. Often too it's marvellously there inside a sentence. "When I lie in bed in the evening I think ever and ever of money and of Kate Creevy." It's the unsaid that makes this sentence go on twisting in the mind.

Only the unsaid can dance with a sentence, and here in the dark they dance all the while.

The silence of the unsaid is always working surreptitiously with another silence, which is that of the unsayable.

What's unsaid one time can be said on another occasion. But the unsayable can never be said – unless maybe in a prayer, and God would know that, not me.

Before the unsayable we are alone. And this, I believe, is why stories are told. All stories are roads which end at a cliff-face. Sometimes the cliff towers above us, sometimes it falls away, sheer at our feet. But when a story leads you to the unsayable, you're in company. That and that alone is the comfort.

The unsaid and the unsayable.

Now let's read the pictures. Black and white photos. Why do photographers – among them some of the best – still persist in taking pictures in black and white, when colour film is so subtle and easy and cheap? Is it a penchant for nostalgia? For asceticism? For morality? Black and white, after all, is mightily moral.

I think it happens for another reason. What does painting do – irrespective of its styles? It invites what isn't there to become present. It starts with what can't be seen. Ask any good painter. Painters study appearances in order to get closer to what lies behind them. Visual art is a chase after the invisible.

The advantage of black and white photos is that they remind you of this search for what can't be seen, for what's missing; never for one moment do they pretend to be complete, whereas colour photos do. There are even colour pictures which are more "finished" than life itself!

By contrast, the black and white portrait of a man in Kerry [page 13] confesses that it can never be finished and against the face of the man from Inishmaan (it's on the preceding page) pound all the high seas of the invisible.

And so they work together, the written lines and the pictures, and they never say the same thing. They don't know the same things, and this is the secret of living together.

The photos are a reminder of everything which is beyond the power of words. Beginning with the first picture of the planks of wood with their grain and their nail and their padlock.

And the words recall what can never be made visible in any photograph. Listen:

> He tells me then he's heard about the music I make with the accordion and I want so badly to play for him to keep him there. He fades in and out like a radio losing its signal.
>
> He leaves the chocolates down beside the bed, and he stands up. He places his large warm hand on my brow and makes a cross like a priest giving the ashes before Lent. "Those people from home, any that remember me tell them I was asking. We're the same you and me. Tell them we forgive them and they should forgive us."
>
> He goes then, the bitter laugh he means for me breaking and falling behind him like a ring of smoke.

Here in the dark you come upon a fusion of the unsayable and the invisible. It sounds tricky that, tricky and vague. But it isn't. Because it's all tattooed on the imagination, point by point, with a needle of longing.

And if you don't think about a book, and you think about a tune? The unsayable, the invisible, the longing in music, they all become clear. They are what music is about. Here is a book of tunes without musical notes. That's why it's a bastard and wrings the heart.

Tunes played in the sad room of a glorious life. *Glorious* is neither irony nor hyperbole here. The word, having travelled the world, goes back to its simple origin: that which has glory.

I'll stay on this page. You go into the room . . .

John Berger

EXILE is not a word
It is a sound
The rending of skin
A fistful of clay on top
       of a coffin
Exile is not a word
It is shaving against
A photograph not a mirror
Exile is not a word
It is hands joined in
       supplication
In an empty cathedral
It is writing your own
       hagiography
It is a continuing atrocity
It is the purgatorial
Triumph of memory
       over topography
Exile is not a word
Exile is not a word

Peter Woods

I COULD READ
THE SKY

1

This room is dark, as dark as it ever gets – the hour before dawn in winter. I have sounds and pictures but they flit and crash before I can get them. The bedclothes are damp. The ache in my neck is bad. I hold onto myself for anchorage.

Something stirs then, a little wind. It's very gentle, a lark's breath, but the thickened air drifts across to clear and I see it – the house set just nicely into the side of the green hill.

The fuchsia bending around the window is red and the thatch so bright you'd think there was a fire in it. I am up on my brother Joe's back painting the north door with my hands. We have the paint but we haven't the brush. The green paint runs down through the little hairs on my arms, under the sleeve of my gansey and onto my chest. But I don't feel it. I am four and Joe is seven. My hands are moving in big, wild loops over the door. There are drips of green on Joe's shirt and the back of his neck. I look into the whorl of brown hair at the back of my head, at my black gansey, my trousers, my blackened feet. The way my face is you'd think there was nothing in the world only the door. I want to climb in behind that face but I can't. I strain to hear some notes of a song from the kitchen. I push at the door. I grip myself tighter.

This is me. I have a round bald head. My eyes are blue and watery and my fingers are stained with tobacco. I am alone here with a black dog. I sleep badly.

The day of the Stations is a big day. The priest will be down in the evening to say Mass in the kitchen and our neighbours and relations will be coming in. We have loaves made. We have chickens cooked. We have whiskey and porter and sherry.

But we forgot about the door.

2

Joe in the kitchen on Stephen's Day got up like a scarecrow. Straw coming out of his sleeves and the neck of his shirt and a pointy hat on him. His face is painted blue. This is his first day hunting the wren and he got ten shillings going around the houses. Mary, Bernadette, Martin, Dermot, Vincent – all out that day. I am in because

I am too young. Eileen is in too. She thinks she's too old to be out with the Wren boys.

I see my father through the window lean his bicycle against the wall. His foot is bad since the fall he took during the potato picking in Lincolnshire. He has a stick to walk with. He's loosened the right pedal on the bike so it stays still while he pushes with his left. He says these days he's getting old and laughs, but he's pushed the bike twelve miles all the way into Ballyconnor and twelve miles back again this Stephen's Day morning. Powerful man. He could put an oar in through the beams of the ceiling and lift himself up over it ten times with each arm. If the foot isn't mended by April when he's to be back in Lincolnshire there'll be no money coming into the house next year.

He comes in through the door, a big smile on him and a canvas bag in his hand. It's like a bag you'd use for cattle feed. There's a coating of snow on the black curls of his head and across his shoulders. His face is sparkling the way water does under a bright sun. Every time I see him limp it makes me want to cry.

He takes Joe over to a chair and lifts the hat off his head. Out from the bag he draws a cardboard box and from the box he takes an accordion, a small single-row Hohner. The shine on it. Marbled red with little stars and a gold trim. He leans over, his face alight, the accordion held like a baby in his big hands – a spalpeen's hands, battered and scarred, the nails split, a finger crushed by a machine. The accordion cost half what you'd get that year for a heifer.

Years later on visits home I'd hunt around under the bed or in the loft for the accordion. But I never could find it. I didn't know it had gone to America with a nephew who couldn't play. Nor that Stephen's Day morning did I know about the fields going to rushes, the fallen walls. I didn't know highways and machines and tunnels and scaffolding. It was a bright day, with the white snow.

Joe takes the accordion from Da and smiles. But he never could play it. The music would come to me, not Joe.

3

"I can't go out the door for fear of that eejit Kane from Mulrany. If I take the bicycle he comes out from behind a hedge. If I go to a dance he ambushes the cart and pushes in beside me. 'If you won't have me,' says he, 'I'll burn your house.' The man is sixty!"

Eileen with Maura Fogarty under my window on a summer evening. I can hear them laughing, high and clear, a sound like small bells. Maybe altar bells. Maura is back from the nursing in England. She wears a dress with little red roses on it and she talks real fast. I am in bed wide awake and I love listening to them.

Matt Doran comes by with his stick and his red dog.

"She's telling me all about the big city, Matt," says Eileen.

"That's a place you wouldn't get a clod of blue clay without paying for it," he says.

He squints then into the last of the sun and moves on.

"What about Jim?" says Maura.

"Gone. His brother sent him the fare. He's in a tannery in Massatuchetts." The way she switched the letters of words around sometimes. It was like Dermot with his wall eye. Or Da's shortened finger. All those things about them would get you when you're alone in the night like this. "After he left Kane came up in his horse and cart to see my Da. Mud all over the spokes. Mud on his boots. He takes off his hat and asks my Da can he marry me. Think of it, passing the

rest of your life with a creature like that. Him with his red nose and his bald head. He's *filthy*, Maura."

"What did your Da say?"

I picture Eileen with the brows scrunched down over her nose. Two caterpillars facing off. Scratches the back of her head with one finger, just like Da. "It's a good farm, girl,' says he. 'Plenty of cows.' But he wouldn't look at me. He knows I'd run away if he made me."

Eileen. If I just think of her voice I can hold it but I cannot find her face, aged eighteen. They all say she was lovely, black hair falling all the way down the length of her back that my father wouldn't let her cut. The last thing he'd say the day he left for Lincolnshire – "And Eileen, please don't cut your hair while I'm away." The hungry way he'd look at you when he was leaving you couldn't refuse him anything.

She cut off her hair that September. In November she started to work for rich people in a house beside a lough to the south. Two years later she was in London.

4

I wait by the door through the nights of this long winter week and then finally I get in. The green paint looks just fine in the evening light. Here in the room the air is neutral, like water in a bath, but inside the house it is warm and loaded. Eggcups full of whiskey. Turf. The glow of the lamp. Chicken bones, the sweat of the dancers, the holy things being put away by the priest. Then Da on the flute, very sweet.

After Da my uncle Eamon gets up from his chair. Everything shining on him. The shoes, the ring, the teeth, the white shirt, his skin. His black hair shines too. He's right next to me and he puts his hand on my shoulder for steadiness. His fingers like Da's are smashed and maimed from the work in England but the only things anyone can ever see are the suit and the shining look of him. He draws a red banknote from his pocket and hands it me.

"Let it be known that henceforth I am to be called by a new name," he says. "There's a man sold me a fine hat in Birmingham goes by the name *Ros-coe*." He put great weight into the word. "That's a name made for me, a name for a man would cut a dash on a city street. Roscoe."

With that he makes two fists, lets out a roar, and from a standing position leaps clean over the table in front of him. Not a glass nor a bottle nor a slice of bread stirs.

He squats down then beside Eileen. "Half a pint of whiskey here!" he calls. Then he takes up Eileen's hands and cranks her arm to get her to sing. "Now girl," he says, "out with your voice."

All their voices. Matt Doran's screech like a goose. The Tailor very low and sombre, like far-off thunder. Da asking Ma for a dance. Ma passing around the sandwiches. The Master giving out a poem about ingratitude. Heaney the Works Inspector down from Dublin played his harmonica and danced, coins and tobacco flying from his pockets. Uncle Roscoe walked once around the room on his hands and then out the door, everyone he passed paying respects to his new name. "Good evening, Roscoe," they'd say. Eileen, her eyes closed, her head back, singing "Róisín Dubh". Joe whispering later in the corner trying to imitate her.

It was a night to remember.

Eileen gets me out for a reel before the thick air closes in again and when I look up with her spinning me round it seems the whole galaxy is whirling above me.

* * *

5

I am up on a high rock above the house in Labasheeda. Nothing behind me only the crest of the hill. The sky has the look of the sea in winter. Then it reddens, clears, and the whole of the valley below me fills with golden light. I turn slowly on the rock.

All the way on the left the Rathangan road taking a turn in under the oaks. Three milk canisters up on the wall beside Matt, his pipe, his stick and his red dog. Tullaherin starting its low rise under his feet. Murran's field, Lally's field. The field where Joe Roddy took a heart attack. The gambling pit. Wisps of purple over the bog. Some say there's bones in it from the Famine. The waterfall, the sparkle and laughter of it. Ma with the hens, her shadow streaking up the lime-stone. Ballinaclash. Ardnageeha. Killycolpy. All the stone walls running over the land like the veins in my hand. John Hall with his pet goose building another wall to nowhere for he's nothing to do. The Tailor in through his window, taking a soft cloth to his loom. Joe Connor arguing with his son under his gable wall. Knocksouna. Glenanaar. What's that Matt said it meant? Glen of the slaughter.

I open my eyes in Kentish Town. Always this neutral air. There is some grey light coming in but it hasn't that cold steely look of the winter sea I could see from the rock. A chair beside the bed. Tablets. A shirt with little blue squares, the collar shot. A bottle of Guinness here and another on the ledge. Maggie's rosary, crystal beads. The paper from

home. The black box with the accordion. A bowl, spoonful of soup in it. A wardrobe made by people I've never met. The grey light crawls up my liver-spotted hands. I hear the dog dreaming in the other room. Is there a kind of sum to this? I wait.

I get back. Dunnamanagh. Cush. Fenit, the wild place. The blackened walls where the Tans burnt out the O'Rourkes. Dunleavy's field where they took the Beggarman to be shot. Kennedy's dog nipping at the cows. Baby pushes

her empty pram out before her from behind Tullaherin, the keys on the string around her neck shining in the light, Matt touching the brim of his cap to her as she passes. "If you ever see her astray on the road, guide her home," he told me. "The mad may be blessed." The well in the long field. Matt says there's a fish in it will tell you how your relations are doing in America. The golden light shines on Kate Creevy, the Tailor's daughter, as she walks down the lane. Blackberries. The MacDonaghs slumped over chairs in their kitchen saying the rosary. I see Dermot and Vincent looking for trout by the river. The coppery haze from the flat rocks in the evening light. Capparoe. Ellistrin. Mullaghareirk. Oola. Dromdorry. Suil.

Labasheeda, the bed of silk.

I turn on the rock.

This is me.

6

The sound of the gun since early morning. Ma says Martin'll have the townland cleared of every living creature by nightfall. She hates the sound of it. "It would put you in mind of the ambushes," she says. But she'll say nothing. He's to pass his last day in Ireland killing all around him with Da's gun.

I cross over to Matt's. His wife's by the fire reading a letter. She's Matt's spectacles down on the end of her nose. He's at the table moving around a parcel from America. The way he picks at it with the tips of his fingers to get it open you'd think it was a sick hen.

"What's the parcel, Matt?" I ask him.

"Tom sent it from Chicago. You'd want to be an engineer to open it."

Two bangs of the shotgun from Martin.

"Martin's away tomorrow," I tell him.

"Martin. A young girl from Killycolpy. John and Patrick, the Tailor's two lads. All for the train tomorrow morning. That leaves only the Tailor himself and Kate at home. I wonder will any of them get as far as Tom in Chicago."

He's the string off now, then the paper. Inside is a box. He opens it with his blade and peers into it. He slips his hands down the sides and lifts out what's inside. A square black shining thing with a crested top. Mesh across the front over hay-coloured cloth and the word "Comet" written over it.

19

Two big dials like owls' eyes. A radio that came all the way from America.

Matt turns the dial with a little click. A light goes on inside and then we hear a voice, very low. Matt looks up from his crouch and winks over to me.

"Here, Maire," he calls. "Tom's sent us a black box from Chicago with a little man inside. He's talking about how it's raining up in Dublin. Let's see does he speak like a Yank."

Matt turns the dial again and the voice crackles and slides. It's like a fiddle tuning up.

Matt cups his hand over his ear, leans over and says, "What's that you said, sir?"

Maire Doran rolls her eyes and goes back to her letter but I can see by the shake of her back that she's laughing.

"Here. Make yourself useful," says Matt, and he hands me over a whistle. I remember Matt like that. The way he'd put on his spectacles and read out from the paper about General Franco. He'd read some lines, look out at us over the rims, and start in again, the voice rising. The face turning to the colour of a strawberry. He couldn't reach the end. "I'll go there and finish the blackguard myself!" he'd say, the paper thrown in a ball into the dust. I remember the little field it took him two years and a thousand creel-loads of sand to build. I remember him standing over his daughter's coffin, those blue eyes that would go into you like spears misting over, a strong man broken. He shouted that night at the sky. I play him "The Pipe and the Hob" before I go.

When I wake the next morning I think tonight there'll be more room in the bed. Martin's already in the kitchen walking around in his new shoes and coat. We're all gathered in to say goodbye to him. The two geese are calling out from the bottom drawer of the dresser. Ma can't stop moving around. Vincent looks like he's cross it's Martin going and not him. Da's pulling up beet in England. Eileen gives Martin a photograph of Ma and Da in an oval wooden frame. Ma gives him a rosary and sandwiches. We shake hands with him, Dermot, Vincent, Joe, myself, then the girls. Brid is with the dog by the fire. She has on a little yellow dress and no shoes. There's the grey powder of turf ash on her feet. Ma goes over to get her to say goodbye to Martin. "Shake hands with your brother now, Brid," she says. Brid wasn't even the length of Martin's leg that time. He bends over with his hand out and she looks up. Her hand goes up but then she stops. She's looking past him to the window by the north door. Everything in her face stops moving until it balls up like a fist when she begins to cry. "Rabbits," she says. We all look to the window. Four dead rabbits upside-down looking in, their feet bound with fishing line. Their stomachs are opened up where Martin gutted them, blood matting the fur. Their mouths are open. Their dead eyes like little shards of coal. "Go on and say goodbye to Martin now, Brid," says Ma. "No!" she says. I feel the pierce of her shriek in my ear. She holds her hands up to her chest and looks away. She'll not touch him nor look at him now.

Martin in New York. Sometimes I'd try to think of the wide avenues straight as drills through the buildings. Big fistfuls of dollars for Martin. One day he fell into a furnace and died.

7

A bottle breaks high on the wall, the pieces of glass falling. Then the screech of a woman, vicious as a cat. She keeps it up under my window until she runs out of breath, then walks on. I picture her fat with long hair in a dirty pink cardigan, white socks on her ankles and rat-like eyes. I was nicely asleep.

I turn on the light. The blister on the wallpaper up by the ceiling and the stain where I tipped over the stout. Maggie's not here now.

Inside the drawer I feel for the pictures and I take them out. Da by the house with a straw hat down over his eye and a grin on him like he's just won at cards. I try to look right into him. Brid with the two old horses and then later in Florida with a big fish. She writes on the back it's called a marlin. I never noticed that before. Dermot's boy in his waiter's gear at the hotel. Maggie raising a glass, the dress with bluebells. Maggie I can't look at very long.

I come to me in the jacket Ma bought me that Fair Day in the town. It had a name written on the lining at the back, I remember. J. Brady. I'm looking straight ahead, creases in my brow and around the mouth where I'm starting to smile, like I'm hearing a joke I know the end of. Lips shining a little somehow. Eyes clear as spring-water. Ma says the high bones and the clear eyes come from island people her side. The face lean down from the bones through to the chin. What I couldn't do then. However

23

did I come to have a head the shape of a television?

The blaze and pop of the photographer's light in his little room above the tobacconist's. Ma watching. I can see nothing only white light until I feel him trying to get me out. He has to lead me by the arm. Brides on the wall. Alice Curran with red hair from Slieverue that Martin walked home one time from a dance. A nun all in white. The carpet is blue but worn to grey at the door. Rooms smell dead in the town.

I turn out the light.

I am walking with Ma up the town after having my photograph taken. Lovely baskets filled with eggs and straw. Crates of butter kept fresh with cabbage leaves. Cakes. Herrings. Mackerel. Dulse. Men with their backs to the wall, smoking. Has no one in the town anything to do? The travelling cinema. There's Lord Masborough's Packard. Every tenant south of the river will be beating birds out of the fields for the next fortnight. Ma stops before a little man with a long neck standing behind a row of tea chests. "Everything for the home and farm." The standings with the cash clothes where Ma bought my jacket. I watch Dermot go by tapping the flank of the Banshee with a stick. She's a wary look in her eye, poor creature. Horses, donkeys and cattle walking up the street. Pens of geese and ducks making a racket. Pigs with their heads low. The animals have taken over the town. I think of a picture I saw of the King of England and a trail of men in plumes and robes and short trousers on Coronation Day.

Peter Egan drives up with a load of turkeys. His shirt is

black with soot from sitting under the chimney all day. My cousin Joe Brennan is standing at the door of a pub.

"How does a thing like that have so many birds?" he asks me.

I tell him all about how the only work Peter Egan will turn to is poaching fish and stealing fowl. I'm glad to be talking to Joe. Peter Egan has a special interest in turkeys, I tell him. He has a son my age told me that old Peter put out a report to the farms beside him that for two nights running he saw a motor car rise up out of the bog into the air with lights blazing, dead people inside roaring to get out and the Man in Black at the wheel. When no one would leave their homes at night he took away all the turkeys he wanted. "Catch them by the beak," he told the lad. "That way they won't call out."

Joe laughs. "You deserve a drink of stout for that," he says, and hands me the glass. I take some, my second taste of it after Uncle Roscoe let me drink from his.

"Where are you for?" I ask him.

"Up the town."

We fall in beside the animals. I look around for Ma and Dermot and when I can't find them I feel a little strange. It seemed that at home everybody always knew where every-

body was. There's sun but it doesn't get to the street because of the buildings. Sometimes it would blind you like the photographer's bulb when it would hit a high window. I've a heifer beside me, a big pig behind. The horses near have to be dragged. The smell of them all together in the air. Kate Creevy in the bakery taking tea with her aunt. Every time I see her it's like I take a blow to the chest.

"When's Dermot getting married?" says Joe.

"February."

"There might be something for you above so."

I don't know what he means. But amn't I something to be

walking up the town with a hard man like Joe? Lads from the town leaning into the wall. "Which are the beasts, the cows or the buff shams?" says one. I remember all the names they called me in Ipswich and Barnstaple and Luton. Joe could take two of these lads one in either hand by the collar and pitch them into the river if he wanted. I know what they do all day in the town. They hold up the walls.

Dermot and the Banshee take a left turn into the square. Once she's taken from there I'll not see her again. Three years cleaning her byre and taking her milk to the creamery. I see the buyers standing under the trees, the farmers leading in their beasts. They look so solemn you'd think it was a procession in church.

Joe keeps on. Outside Neeson's public house at the end of the town nine young lads and three girls are standing before four farmers in their jackets and caps. Another drives up and joins them. There's Jerry Blake, Patsy O'Hagen, Dan O'Driscoll. Mary and Philomena Sweeney from Tobermoney. I don't know the others. Joe and I stand in with them. I hear the buyers making offers in the square. The farmers are having a great gawk at us all from near and far. I wonder what the Banshee will bring and who will take her. Joe walks over to talk to the farmer who came up on his pony and trap. I look over to the square to see is Dermot coming out. When I turn back there's a man before me. He's thin lips and stains of porter at the corners of his mouth. He hasn't shaved, an orangey-red stubble covering his jaw. His face is so fat you can barely see his eyes. Ma takes a dim view of men who don't shave.

"Can you mind horses and cattle?" he says.

"I can."

"Can you cut turf?"

"I can."

"Can you operate machines?"

"I can."

"Would ten shillings and your bed and board do you?"

"It would I suppose."

"All right so," he says. "Come to this place tomorrow morning."

He hands me an old envelope with his name and address on it. I stand in the road holding it. Joe gets up in the seat beside the man in the pony and trap. Everyone begins to move away. Dermot must still be in the square trying to sell the Banshee. I hope he makes a good job of the place now it's his for I dearly wanted it for myself.

8

Water drips from the roof down into the stone tank beyond the wall. The notes of water hitting water hold under the sheet of tin he's put over the tank. I heard a sound like it this afternoon on an electronic machine in the Gloucester Arms. They must get those sounds somewhere. The wall is damp and the floor is damp. You couldn't walk on it without shoes. She's given me a candle but no lamp. A Sacred Heart on the wall, the glass broken. A chair. That's

broken too. A paper bag with my spare shirt. Mrs Casey keeps the jacket Ma bought me in a wardrobe inside. What was it lived here before me, hens or pigs?

The work is very stale for no one talks. They measure seven cups of water into the kettle for tea and two thin slices of bread each. I get three potatoes and no butter with dinner. They have a number for everything they give out and it's always small. I've to eat in the barn. He's near 180 acres and three men apart from the three sons. Joe said after I'd been hired I should have gone with a small farmer.

There's a place beyond to walk to called the Doctor's

Dam. Some terrible thing happened to a doctor in it so no one goes near it. I don't know the names of places here. The hired girl who works with Mrs Casey in the house won't look at me when she speaks.

When I lie in bed in the evening I think ever and ever of money and of Kate Creevy. What is the distance between me and her? I see her walking ahead of me in the town. She's a basket on her arm and she's wearing a hat. A hat! It wasn't Sunday. She's a long stride but it's very light. I can see the line of her leg under her skirt. Sometimes her foot turns on a stone in the path and she has to right herself. I'd be there to catch her if she fell. She has gloves on a colour grey like a pigeon's breast. Her hair pinned up, the sweep of it over her ear, the long lines of her neck. The heartbeat is booming in

my head. I take the tin box out from under the bed. £1 2s. 6d. I lost a pound on a Sunday in the gambling pit. I begin to count. I can put four shillings in the box each week. Times four. Sixteen shillings. Times twelve. £9 12s. for the year. I give names to the numbers as I think of them. Bonham. Blade. Set of delft. Horse. Black frieze coat to keep her warm. Whitewash. Barrel of porter. Bed. What is the distance between me and her? She stops and looks down at her foot. The black bootlace a scrawl in the dirt of the road. She lifts her foot up to a ridge in the wall and lifts her skirt away

from the boot. She lifts it so that the edge of it rests on her knee. The skin of her leg is the colour of a peach. I see her fine bones moving as she balances. Her mouth is open a little. The long line of her neck. Her fingers as she works the laces. Small bones like the bones of hens moving in her hands. What matter, I had Maggie all those years. But not then. The thought of Kate Creevy. I could circle the whole of her ankle with my hand. When I reach her by the wall she leaves her skirt where it is on her knee. She looks up. The green of her eyes. Flecks of gold. How can I speak? The

words turn inside out in my head. The distance. I walk with her a little way along the road. I take in all the air around her. My chest is on fire. Would I take her in Casey's cart to the station so she can visit her sister in Dublin? Her father's refused. It's the Gaoler he should be called, she says, not the Tailor. I would, I say. You're a good friend, she says. The distance between me and her. I rattle the tin box. There's no horse nor farm nor bonham nor bed in it. The distance. Wouldn't a dog be a friend like that?

9

What I could do.

I could mend nets. Thatch a roof. Build stairs. Make a basket from reeds. Splint the leg of a cow. Cut turf. Build a wall. Go three rounds with Joe in the ring Da put up in the barn. I could dance sets. Read the sky. Make a barrel for mackerel. Mend roads. Make a boat. Stuff a saddle. Put a wheel on a cart. Strike a deal. Make a field. Work the swarth turner, the float and the thresher. I could read the sea. Shoot straight. Make a shoe. Shear sheep. Remember poems. Set potatoes. Plough and harrow. Read the wind. Tend bees. Bind wyndes. Make a coffin. Take a drink. I could frighten you with stories. I knew the song to sing to a cow when milking. I could play twenty-seven tunes on my accordion.

10

I lift the flap of hide over the gap in the wall. The gap is not much bigger than the size of a fist but light falls through it onto the pig. He looks up at me from the ground, eye to eye. The pig's eye is like the eye of the priest. Very calm and sure. I am no longer sure of anything. Looking at the eye of the pig with his blond lashes you'd think he could do sums quicker than you. The eye of the horse makes you warm. The eye of the cow makes you sad. The eye of the sheep makes you think you might grow stupid just looking at it.

I go out into the road to have a look around. Tom Connor's new wife is hanging up sheets on the line. Wherever did he get a fine girl like that? He keeps pigs in the wreck of a motor car. The postman glides up on his bicycle. He's something for the Connors, for us and for Matt, but he passes by the Tailor. The Tailor is in the doorway in his underwear. He hasn't anything on his feet and his hair is standing on his head. He steps out of the gloom of his house a little way into the yard. He hasn't whitewashed the house since Kate left. He shakes his fist at the back of the postman. "Fuck you!" he shouts. "Fuck you and fuck your bicycle!" There's a line of spittle on his chin. He goes back into the house. Matt says he sleeps on a chair in the kitchen under newspapers.

Matt crosses the road carrying his long blade and we go back into the yard. Matt says he's lost track of where I am now. I tell him a family named Keenan out the Ballyconnor road. "If you owned all the acres you've worked you'd be as rich as Lord Masborough," he says. Ma is washing down the table in the centre of the yard. Mary is filling the stan Joe Connor and his brother brought over with water and salt. Dermot comes out, then Da. Da has a bottle of whiskey with him. He winks over to Matt and leaves it down on the window-ledge. Brid is in the fields for the last time she saw the white carcass of a pig hanging in the turf house she thought it was a ghost.

Dermot lets the pig out into the run. The eye isn't so calm now that it sees all of us. Da makes a lunge at him but falls

in the dirt. He's slow to pick himself up while the others make grabs at the pig. There's a rattling down in Da's lungs. He rubs his shoulder where he fell on it. He looks around and laughs but I can see when I look in his eye that he's lost. He's a red shirt on with the sleeves rolled up. The power in his arms. His smile in the photograph with the straw hat. He could smile like he owned the world and would give it all away. Why didn't I help him to his feet? Why didn't I ask him who he was?

I have hold of the pig around the middle. When I used run my hand along his flank he'd lie down like a dog. His heart is going off like small bombs in the massiveness of his chest. Matt has him by the ears, Joe Connor by the tail. Dermot gets the grin around his snout and tightens it. Da pushes from behind. We heave him up onto his back on the table, Da and Dermot at the back legs, Joe Connor and his brother Tom at the front, me holding back the head. The pig is making more noise than the whole of a city. Matt with his blade in his hand looks around at everybody and says as he always does that the pig is the only animal can see the wind. Then he cuts a Sign of the Cross into the throat of the pig. "Now," he says to me. "If you can find all the notes in 'Lord Gordon's Reel' you can find the aorta of the pig." He hands me the blade.

The day I found Joe in the abattoir in Ipswich. Men with white hats kicking pigs and putting paper numbers on their backs. Blood running down the white tiles. I put my fingers in my ears against the pigs' screaming, some down on the floor given up, others running over them in the pens. The smell of death dense in the air like clots. There's a man beating pigs with sticks towards their deaths. There's a man putting hooks through their heels so they can be hung upside-down. There's a man sending currents through their brains. Where's Joe? Con said he'd heard he was sleeping in the bushes in Hyde Park. Another that he'd gone on the Merchant Marine out of Glasgow. And another that he had a big family in Birmingham. It was Pat Creevy told me about the abattoir. I walk through the white room covered with blood. The thud of the electric shocks. The boiling water. The sound of the saw splitting carcasses. In a cubicle at the end of the room, astride a grate, covered in sheets drenched in blood, a long blade in his hand, is Joe. The hooked pigs move along on a chain in the air and when they stop before him he sticks them. He waits while the pigs empty themselves through the grate. He cuts no Sign of the Cross into their throats. We have crubeens and bottles of stout in his room that night but when I go to see him a month later he's gone.

Joe Connor sings "The Rocks of Bawn" while Ma fries the griskins and pig's liver in butter. The bottle of whiskey is half empty. In Joe's voice there is more than one sound. There's a deep drone like from the pipes and above it pure sweet notes. You never know until he sings them where they'll come from. A stone dropped in a well. Rocks forming in the earth. How does Joe know so much about the hurt of this man with land that cannot be ploughed? I have a sound on the accordion I know is mine but that I cannot yet reach. It seems red and gold and full of light. It's fast and sure.

We eat the meat from the pig. I think of his trotters pawing at the air like he's trying to run as the blood pumps out of the wound I made into the basin. When we finish Matt orders more music. Da plays a tune on the flute, then me on the accordion. We play a pair of reels together. Then Matt calls on me to play "The Moving Cloud". I have some whiskey in me. There's something about the way Matt is tapping his foot and cocking his head, the way he draws the music into him this night. He's like a man with a plate of stew after a long day in the fields. When I hit the first notes

my hands take off like a pair of birds. I can feel the tune spilling itself out inside me. I can see all the notes like they're small coloured stones you'd find on the strand. I can look at all sides of them and find the right place for them to go. I could go to the well and back between each of them. Ma sits down by the fire. Mary leaves down the plate she was washing. Brid comes in from the yard. I've never been in this place before but I know all about it. Da is watching my hands. I could keep them flying for a month. I finish the tune and put the accordion down onto the floor. The kitchen

seems to ring as though the tune is leaving slowly. Then it's quiet. "You've never played like that before," says Matt, "and maybe you never will again." Da goes to the table and pours out a whiskey for himself and me, then hands the bottle to Joe Connor. He brings me the glass. He looks like he's just had another child. "You've passed me out now," he says. "It was time for you."

11

Something moves in the kitchen and I wake up. It sounds like the leg of the table against the floor. All night I've slept for ten minutes and then lain awake for an hour. I wonder is my ticket for the train in my pocket or in the drawer. Light comes in from the kitchen under the bottom of my door. I can see a pair of shoes and the edge of my suitcase.

I go out into the kitchen. Da is lying on the floor in front of the fire with his arm around a sleeping calf. He looks up.

"What's wrong?" I ask him.

"Swollen navel," he says.

He lies back down with the calf then.

12

I open my eye. First there's the dryness. I can't get anything to move in my mouth for it's stuck. Then the pain. It's like there's a small animal with feet made of fire running inside my head. Then the feelings of poison and of shame. I look at the grey pillow, the coverlet, pink wearing away. It was a colour Maggie liked on some things. There'll be no comfort in the bed this morning.

I was, let me see, five hours in the Gloucester Arms yesterday evening. I went in at five and came out at ten. What else am I to do after I've walked the dog? I must have said something to the Greek over the game of dominoes for when he left he never spoke to me. I was out the door and down the road before I remembered I'd left the dog tied to a leg of the chair. I had nine pints and a cheese sandwich. Strange white cheese I never ate before. I can't take the drink the way I did.

On the first day I thought England was all grey walls running with water.

When the boat pulls into the harbour we put away our instruments and fold up the chairs. The big iron doors they left open to give us air draw closed, the grey water churning. The sky looks like pork gone off. The noise of the engine crashes through the hold. The lorries are dark and still as cows waiting for rain. There were six of us playing tunes like we were all raised under the same roof, and another thirty maybe watching. We go up onto the deck to have a look at England, the vile taste of the tea they gave us on the boat still with me. If you could see the brightness on their faces when the tunes were playing you could see nothing now. Just the look of waiting. The look of people waiting in a hospital.

We glide in silence through the docks. Rust. The walls pitted and streaked with green slime, water running down them. The lock gates open before us and then we rise up the walls. The lock is a pure marvel to me but I can't think why it's needed. We stop. The lock is like a tomb. A girl with black hair and a blue raincoat, face very pale, is gripping the rails. She has her suitcase between her legs. Her eyes are

wide and she's pulling at the air. It's like she's drowning. The sound of it is all we can hear as we wait in the water. She doesn't seem to know what's happening to her. I want to go to her but I don't. Then when the boat rises again in the lock she seems to be all right.

We go out through the gate towards the dock. There's a newspaper, a child's doll in a pink dress and the tyre of a motor car in the water. The doll is missing an arm. We all walk out onto the dock with our suitcases. If anyone's thinking twice about where they're going they're letting on nothing. I look around without any reason to see is anyone

here to meet me. The wind is blowing hard and it surprises me. I always thought it would be dead calm. I think of a wind at home that had such force it lifted a cat and threw it over a wall. Everyone scatters, but a young lad named John Joe who played the mouth organ goes with me to the train. A long tunnel, the dark walls sweating an oily kind of water. Then the high cuttings as we pass out of the city. Black bricks, moss and streaks of water. I am in England now.

I roll over onto my side. The wardrobe door is open, Maggie's dress with the bluebells hanging there. It's the only thing I won't give away. What had I with me when I stepped out onto the docks? A suitcase of clothes. The accordion. The note Da gave me to tell me where to go. £4 6s. I'd saved and Ma's £2, that was £6 6s. What have I now? I look for my trousers. They're in a heap on the floor where I walked out of them last night. I'll have to put some order into the place. £1.27 in the pocket. And the pension won't arrive until Thursday. What will I do today? I'll lie in bed thinking of the grey walls of Liverpool running with water.

The day I left Da went out very early with the sick calf and wouldn't come near the house. Ma fries me two lovely eggs she brought in that morning. She gives me a rosary and sandwiches. She goes to the press, takes out a box and hands me £2. It's a fine little box made of pine that was full of cigars when Martin sent it to Da from New York. That winter when the men came visiting at night they lay on their backs on the stone floor with their feet to the fire and smoked cigars instead of pipes.

I ate the last of the sandwiches waiting to get on the boat at the North Wall. I kept the £2 until I forgot which ones they were. I put the rosary into the coffin with Ma.

I go to the door and look for Da. He has a sheep up on his back and he's walking away from the house past the well. He tips his hat to Baby just like Matt as she labours up a small hill with her pram. "It's well for her she's in Labasheeda," he'd say, "for the city would crush her." I hope he won't fall under the weight of the sheep. Ma goes to put the sandwiches in my suitcase but the lock snaps open and my clothes spill out onto the floor. She runs a length of twine around it. Dermot brings the cart and we head out the

road. The sun pours through a gap in the clouds and lights up the townland. All the colours of Ma's shawl as she rests against the white wall. Her hair red and going to white some places, her fingers red too from work. The fuchsia and the new thatch, the emerald fields ringed in grey. The clouds close over as we head out. A photograph.

I stand up in the cart and look for Da but I can't find him. He'll be behind a hedge maybe, watching. What did I do along this road? I drove cattle. I hid from the Master. I danced a hornpipe. I waited for Da to come home from Lincolnshire. One day I'll come back along it in a new suit filled with banknotes.

Dermot leaves me down at the station like I was a sack of grain and turns the horse away. I watch after him but he doesn't look back. He takes his cap off and makes a swat at a bluebottle and I see a circle of bare skin the size of a florin at the back of his head. That's the first I ever saw of it. I fear for my own hair then. I run my hand through it but it feels all right. Would I find a fine-looking woman in the dance-halls of England before the hair lets me down?

Cornelius Breen is on the platform with his Ma and Da and sister Agnes. His Ma gets thirty dollars every month from his brother Paul in Philadelphia and maybe six pounds from Declan who's working on roads in England. She's a coat with fur around the collar she had sent up from Dublin. They widened the house to make a parlour and they have the priest in for tea. She's been running a campaign this past year with Cornelius to get him out from beside the fire and into the world making money but he wasn't having any of it.

Matt calls him the Potato That Was Boiled Too Long, for he's soft. His Ma bought him a suitcase. Then she bought him a suit. Good investments, she thought, but still he wouldn't shift. Finally she said she'd give him twelve pounds and the price of his ticket along with it and he agreed. The Da's there with his cap off and a sorrowful look on him like he's at the side of a grave. I can see the smoke from the train. I look over to the bench where I sat with Kate Creevy. Cornelius's Ma starts to cry. "Don't leave me, son," she says, reaching out her arms. I suppose she thought she had to. The train is upon us now. "Don't leave me, Cornelius," she says again. "All right, Ma," says Cornelius, "I won't refuse you," and he walks back to the cart, throws his suitcase into it and sits down. Ma told me in a letter that he was three days in the town drinking away all the money she gave him.

The click of the wheels on the tracks. It sounds different in England. Heavier maybe. Warrington. Manchester. Stockport. Rows of tiny houses joined up together. Sheds out the back with bicycles and mattresses and trunks up on the roof. John Joe's talking to me the whole way about the tunes of Leitrim and the uncle that could play them all on his fiddle. I can see a woman frying fish in a pan. Her hair looks like it's made of wood. The great rush on them all when they get to the stations. What will they sound like? What way will I talk to them?

I take out the bit of paper Da gave me. "The Duke of Cumberland, Lincoln", it says. It's wearing away from all the times I've looked at it since leaving home. I fold it again and put it away into my pocket. What would Da be doing now?

52

Maybe looking out over the land, the sun lighting up his face. The pale girl with the black hair who was unwell on the boat is by the window across from John Joe and me, looking poorly again. She has a handkerchief up to her lips. I see on the floor under her seat a little pool, mostly tea, where she's been sick. She hasn't anyone with her. A huge tall man in a railway uniform comes into the carriage. He's a red beard, a nose like a baby tomato, and eyes as red as the inside of a mouth. The hat is sitting back on his head so you can see the whole of his face. He pulls up when he sees the

sick on the floor. He looks right, and then left. He looks straight at the girl. "Who made this mess?" he says. His voice booms and rattles. The whole carriage is silent and watching. The girl is shaking now. She lifts her hand up to her mouth like she'll be sick again. But he keeps his stare on her. Then John Joe throws his coat over the back of the seat and pushes the sleeves of his gansey as high as they'll go. Christ, the arms on him! They'd collapse a bull. "I did," says John Joe. Your man wheels around. John Joe looks right into his eye, the arms across his chest like two logs. I look into his eye too but then turn away for it's like looking at rancid meat. Everything is moving in John Joe's jaw and neck and arms. His right leg is going up and down like he's marking time to a reel. He's looking right at your man and smiling. One brush of a feather and he'd go off like a land mine. It's like the air is made of glass, John Joe and your man eye to eye. "Don't do it again," says the railwayman and moves off down the carriage, beat. The door slams behind him. John Joe winks at the girl. She laughs, high and light. She laughs in a way that I think she didn't expect.

I was with John Joe until Chester, and then I got onto another train to Sheffield. The names I never took to. There isn't much movement in them and they are closed off at both ends. They remind me of iron. John Joe hadn't a clue where he was going and neither did I. "Where'd you get arms like that?" I said to him before I got off. "I'm a plasterer," he said. "You get them from holding the hawk."

Inside the Duke of Cumberland, sitting at a high stool at the bar, a cigarette burning away in his hand and a pint and the paper from home before him, is P . J. Doran, Matt's nephew. His hair is slicked down with oil. Christy Mangan, Dick Lally, Conor Dowd and his brother Peter, Jimmy Burke and Dan Ryan are all in a gloomy corner playing cards. The last time I saw Dan he was coming up from the quay with two lobster pots and the wind nearly blowing him back into the sea. A Kerryman name of Florrie Clifford I recognised from a photo Da showed me is making his way to the bar. I'd been two hours in the streets of Lincoln looking for the place. I was afraid to speak in case I'd be jeered at. The handle of the case nearly opened a wound in my hand. I all but fall on them when I see them.

It is here that I mix up the money Ma gave me. They fire pints at me but there is no food. They're pints of bitter topped with brown ale. I play them "The Good-Natured Man", "The Whistler from Rosslea" and "The Humours of Tulla". The money drains from my pocket. When I come out of the Gents I trip over the step at the door and open a gash on the bridge of my nose. I look at myself in the mirror until I stop the blood. There's a reel in my head. I have to keep a grip on the basin. I have trouble believing it's myself looking back at me.

Then I am in a car. An Englishman I've never seen before is driving. The men are breathing like cows from all the drink. They tell me there's an old lad from Tyrone who is too weak to pick potatoes any more so they'll put him up on the tractor and I can take his place in the gang. I know nothing of what is to happen to me but I ask no questions. We drive in the darkness out of the city and along the lanes of the countryside of Lincolnshire, houses and hedges and trees thrown behind us with our speed, the sky growling like a dog watching something he doesn't like. P. J. whistles "James Connolly". We get out then and I follow them up a muddy path towards a dark shape. Peter Dowd slips and slides down the slope on the arse of his trousers. How was it I was so incurious about what was to become of me? The drink maybe. More likely the fear of being shamed somehow.

We come then to a door in a building made of stone. The

door is black, the paint flaking, and is held closed by twine stretched between two nails. We are at some kind of an outbuilding on a farm. I am feeling cold while we wait for P. J. to unwind the twine and let us in. The door opens and we file in silently. Where are we going? Inside there is heat and movement and the air thickened with some kind of life. P. J. lights a lantern hanging from a nail in the wall. Stretched in front of me now I see pigs. The room is filled with pigs from one end to the other. The men move towards a length of wooden stair that reaches from the dust of the floor to a hole in the ceiling. The pigs watch us as we make our ascent.

Above in the loft there are twelve sleeping places made of straw along the two walls, with a wash-basin on a stand below a tiny window at the gable end. P. J. hangs the lantern on a nail and points to where I should sleep. The men are making ready for bed, but I stand still at the top of the stairs. I can taste the brine of tears coming into my mouth. My breath is short and the blood seems to be moving at such speed within me that I think I might be thrown to the floor. But I let on nothing. The pigs are moving below. I am standing above them taking in their breath. I feel in my pockets. I wonder have I the fare home and if I can find the way. I think of the bed I left in Labasheeda. Outside it is dark and the road full of twists I know nothing of. There is no way back now. I am to pick potatoes and lie down at night in this loft. I am to be in England living with pigs.

13

I think of the potatoes as made of mud. Or wax. Or dead leaves. If I look up from the ground I'm picking them from the field seems to stretch forever before me. It would be the size of four farms at home maybe. It's November and coming out from under the covers in the morning is like entering the cold sea, but the work is so fierce we have our shirts off by mid-morning. The field is all mud. There's mud on my trousers, mud on the sack and mud up my arms. There's mud gone down into my boots. If I hold a potato in my hand I can make no sense of it. I try to think of a piece of it buttered and salted at the end of a fork. But I can't.

The Yorkshireman comes in full of drink and pisses into the mouth of a pig. I can hear him roaring about it below.

I am in the bed. I can't move, my arms and back and my legs still flaming from the work. P. J. is sitting in the bed beside mine reading a book about astronomy. I am thinking a little hazily of the lovely flowers on the half-acre of potatoes at home. Then I think of the big field we'll face in the morning. How many potatoes for a shirt, a ring, a nice gold watch for Ma? How many before I'd have something to say to Kate Creevy if ever I met her on the road? How many did Da pick to get the accordion for Joe?

P. J. snaps shut the book and leaves it down beside the bed. "I can't think how God can have a spare thought for us with all that's going on in the universe," he says.

He tries to look out through the little window at the night sky.

"Did my father ever work this farm, P. J.?" I ask him.

"No. But he worked at Appleforth's, just two miles to the east. I was there with him. He was great at the hay-making because of the strength in his arms. How's he keeping?"

"Because of the leg Dermot has to do all the work. That bothers him. But my mother says he's started teaching the flute to a young lad named Wilson comes in to him on a bus from eleven miles away. He's the son of a Protestant minister."

"It was an awful shame about the leg."

"What was he like that time?"

"He loved the card school on a Sunday. He couldn't get enough of it. Sometimes I'd see him putting a pile of money in and I'd try to caution him. He had a saying for that. He'd look up at me and wink and say, 'You have to speculate to accumulate.'"

I am lying very still for there's nowhere that I don't feel pain. I try to think of how I'll look coming up the road towards home when I've money saved. I look at myself from all the angles.

"I would love to have a telescope," says P. J.

He is up on one elbow now studying the sky. I never saw him from this side before, where I couldn't get a look at his eyes. He looks older that way.

"How long have you been working in this country, P. J.?" I ask him.

"Seventeen years this past June."

"What's it like?"

He keeps looking out the window for a while, then he turns back and puts out the lantern. I don't know if he's heard me. I can hear him settling down in the straw.

"It's like you're trying to talk to somebody out of a deep black hole," he says.

14

To the south is Orion. Across I find the Plough, the Seven Sisters, the Bear. There's Venus, with a very white star above, and Cassiopeia. The wide streak of the Milky Way like an exploded spine. Lyra, Pegasus. I am sitting against the wall of the pigshed smoking a Woodbine and thinking about the mathematics of space as taught me by P. J.

Dick Lally comes up with such a light step I don't notice he's there until he's beside me. He doesn't speak much but his mouth is nearly always open. His lips are wet and he has the eyes of a child, or an old woman whose mind is gone. The work is hard on him, poor man, and his back is bad.

"Look at what the brother sent me today in a box."

He holds up a small glass bottle with a cork in it filled with a clear liquid, sparkling very gently in the starlight.

"It's not from Lourdes."

He pours out two glasses and we follow the hot track of the poitín as it runs down our throats.

"John O'Hagen's still producing it, Martin tells me. He has the worm right inside the house. I saw him doing it once when I was a lad, all the men standing around staring at the drip-dripping of the poitín as it fell into the bottles. It was like they were watching a cow calve."

Conor Dowd's taken to calling Dick "The Jacket" since the right sleeve ripped open up to his oxter. It's blackened at

the elbows and blackened where it falls onto his hips. It has one button in front and none on the sleeves. There's a tear up the back and he has that one and the one on the arm fixed with pins.

He shifts a little where he sits in the dirt and pours us each another glass.

"I wonder would you ever do us a small favour," he says.

He looks at me with those eyes.

I would of course, I tell him.

"It's because of the letter from Martin," he says. "He had some bad news for me. You can see for yourself. It's Sheila.

You know the way it is with me and the writing. You'll know what to say to her."

He tells me what he wants said and leaves me the letter from his brother. Then he goes back into the shed.

Dear Sheila, I wrote. I enclose one guinea from this week's pay together with an extra two bob for each of the two girls so they can have something special for Hallowe'en. How are they, and yourself? It's a long while since I've heard from you. My health is holding up and even the back is not too bad, thank God. All the men from home are also well. P. J. is talking about a big roadworks near Birmingham and some of the lads are thinking of going on there when the taties are finished, but I want to be back for Christmas to be with you and the girls. Sheila, I had news from Martin today that disturbs me greatly. He says Brendan Flannery has been around to the house nearly every day since June. He says he's seen the two of you walking in the lane in the evening. He says he thinks there's something between you that's not right, Sheila. The whole of Oola is talking about it, he says. I never thought such a thing could happen to us, Sheila. You mean the world to me, you and the girls. When I'm here on the farm I'm thinking ever of us all together in Oola. I know it's hard to be the wife of a spalpeen, but it's for yourself and the girls that I came here. I would love for you to tell me that it isn't so. I would love to find out it's a lie or a bad dream, but I fear the worst. Now I have to ask you, Sheila, is the child that's coming before Christmas mine, or is it Brendan Flannery's? I love you with all my heart. Your loving husband, Conor.

15

When I hear about the death of Roscoe I am washing my socks and thinking about the way Da played "Anach Cuain" on his flute. He'd always get great silence when he played it because he'd lift the flute very slowly, draw it up to his mouth, close his eyes and wait for a beat of five

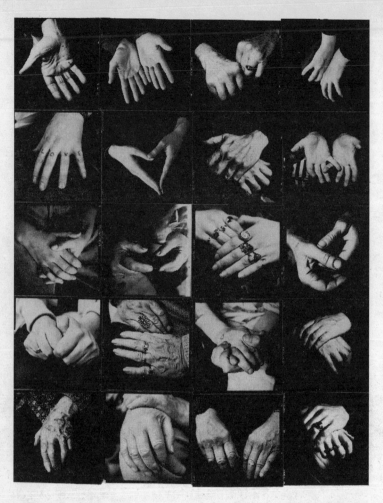

before he made the first note. At the start it would be light, slow and gentle, almost faint, like the first smoke rising from kindling. Then he'd build it. It was best when he was sitting in a chair on his own against the yellow wall, for you'd want to see only him. But then everything was away anyway once he was into the tune. He'd drive the whole world away with his music. As he built the tune you would feel it moving into you, twisting and curling like a wild vine running on a wall. The face would never change. The eyes down. Maybe once you'd see a flicker across the brow. I'd heard the tune since before I could walk but I never knew where the next note would come from. Always it seemed a surprise. But it was as right and sure as the flight of a hawk. At the height of it you were away too. You were only music. When he finished the world would come back again but it was different. Whatever it is that has us walking in the world but not noticing it was away. Everything around was on you like a storm.

Conor Dowd comes in and tells me he's heard Roscoe died in a pipe by the side of a road near Brighton. It was a big pipe waiting to be put underground. Roscoe was in the gang and seemingly he couldn't get digs. He was living in the pipe. They found him dead there in the morning.

"We are the immortals," says P. J. He has a few jars on him. "We have one name and we have one body. We are always in our prime and we are always fit for work. We dig the tunnels, lay the rails and build the roads and buildings. But we leave no other sign behind us. We are unknown and unrecorded. We have many names and none are our own. Whenever the stiffness and pain come in and the work gets harder, as it did for Roscoe, we change again into our younger selves. On and on we go. We are like the bottle that never empties. We are immortal." He lays down into his bed then and lets out a long sigh.

"I'm awfully sorry about Roscoe," Conor says to me. "He was a gas man. He could make up a limerick in two seconds."

There was no lament for Roscoe. I like to think of Da standing by the side of his grave, drawing out his flute and playing "Anach Cuain" over the coffin. The way he could make the ache of it so beautiful. I hear "Anach Cuain" sometimes when I go to sleep. Then if I wake in the middle of the night it's still there.

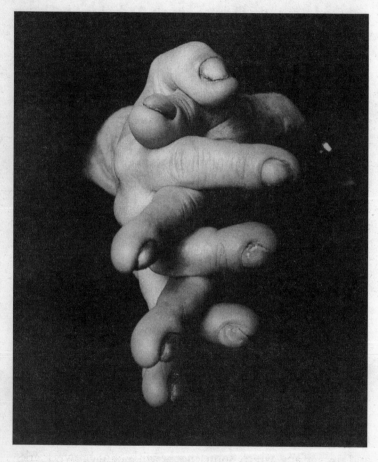

16

What I couldn't do.

Eat a meal lacking potatoes. Trust banks. Wear a watch. Ask a woman to go for a walk. Work with drains or with objects smaller than a nail. Drive a motor car. Eat tomatoes. Remember the routes of buses. Wear a collar in comfort. Win at cards. Acknowledge the Queen. Abide loud voices. Perform the manners of greeting and leaving. Save money. Take pleasure in work carried out in a factory. Drink coffee. Look into a wound. Follow cricket. Understand the speech of a man from west Kerry. Wear shoes or boots made from rubber. Best P. J. in an argument. Speak with men wearing collars. Stay afloat in water. Understand their jokes. Face the dentist. Kill a Sunday. Stop remembering.

17

I turn all the way around and look at the men. They are kneeling, their heads bent over their flat caps and their rosaries. I cannot see the faces of any of them, but Matt is there for I know his shape well. Their heads are very still. The heads are like the eggs of a giant bird balanced in a line along the back pew. The skin on their heads is dry and papery and white, some maybe with faint brown marks from age. You would only see this skin when the men are in church or in their beds for at all other times they are in their caps.

Between the men and me are the people of the parish. They do not shift on their knees or whisper or cough the way they would at an ordinary Mass. Their eyes are on the priest. If anyone sees I am watching them their heads drop slowly before rising again to the altar. The faces of young lads and girls who were children when I left now have angle and shape. In their eyes instead of simplicity there is sureness or doubt or preoccupation. In the eyes of Sarah McCabe there is a look of awakening. The eyes of my Aunt Rosemary hold tears.

These are the people who saw Da from the time of his birth. They saw him by the river. They saw him play his flute. They saw him courting. They saw the arc of his strength rising and falling. Some were with him in the fields of England. You can see in the look of all of them the weight of their work and the weight of those around them being born and dying. If I could see past that look inside into their heads I would take out all that they ever saw of Da and make it into a long movie I could watch. I would watch him dance. I would watch him on the deck of a boat. I would watch him walking in the lane with Ma when they were young.

Between the people in the pews and the men kneeling in the back is the young Protestant boy was taking lessons from Da in the flute. He wears a black suit with not a crease to be seen in it and a black tie with gold stripes. His fair hair is combed very neatly across the top of his head. He has the look of being asleep with his eyes open. His arms are out

before him and he is holding Da's flute. Before the priest says his prayers over the coffin the boy is to walk up the aisle and leave the flute down on top of the lid.

I look now at the coffin with Da inside. I can see the shine on the nails which seal him in. I think of a question and I turn to ask him. I think of what I saw in England and how I can describe it to him. I think of a tune I want to play for him. The way the wind moves through the wall and blows the leaves over the stones, the way the priest speaks the prayers, the way Dermot's shoulders are drawn down to the ground, they are all like this because he is gone. Ma is looking at the priest like she can read the future on his face. Her lips are tight, almost white, her eyes pinched. She could be carved from ice. He is gone from the world, we are thinking. I think too as I sit by his coffin that I will never again have such respect for a living person and now that he is no longer here I will not be able to stop things falling from their places. A sadness reaches like a clawed hand into my bones and organs. It fills the spaces between. It is heavy and strong. I believe that this sadness can never leave me.

The priest comes down to the foot of the altar and nods his head at the back of the church. I turn again and look back at the boy. He begins to walk forward. The way his legs move it's like he's stepping over uncertainly balanced stones in a stream. Once a week he left his father's vicarage and travelled eleven miles on the bus to Da to learn to play the flute and eleven miles back again in the evening. Da was amazed by him, Ma says, by his seriousness, by the way he asked about the music, by the way he held the flute when he went to play. You'd think it was a holy relic, Ma says. Da talked about him through the week and waited on his arrival. I look at the boy's eyes. They still seem to have the look of sleep on them. The whole of the church is watching him. His eyes go then onto the coffin and grow wide. He breathes in like he can't quite catch the air. His right leg seems to go from under him, he opens his mouth and he says the word "I". His voice is high and sweet. It sounds like the beginning of a song. This is the love he has for Da. He begins to fall then. Hands reach out to him and he tries to right himself by grabbing at the pews. But he can't. As he falls I see on his face his look of unconsciousness and grief. A fine stream of blood runs from his top lip as he lies on the wooden floor of the church. The flute rolls from his hand down the aisle towards the coffin.

18

When the Tailor comes to the door he's eating a raw potato. His underclothes are all one piece, reaching to his wrists and his ankles. The buttons are open. You can see the lines of the bones in his chest. Hair grows over his eyes, from his nose and across his face like rushes overtaking a disused field. He blinks his eyes in the light. There's a kind of terror in them.

"Is it you?" he asks me.

"It is."

"What ails you?" There's a shrillness to his voice like he might cry or as though he fears the answer might harm him.

"I would like a suit."

"A suit?"

"A suit for Mass and for travelling and for attending dances."

He looks into my face like I've asked him a riddle. Then finally he speaks.

"All right so," he says.

Inside the house smells of fallen trees soaked with water. It is dark, just a small oil lamp burning. Newspapers cover the windows. Over a picture of the Pope with a gold frame he's taped a handkerchief, but you can still see the veined and ringed hands folded together. The dresser, a table and chairs are pushed into a corner with a sheet thrown over them. There's a harness and a small plough. By the fire, his

chair, with newspapers for blankets. The loom stands alone in the centre of the room, not a trace of dust to be seen on it, the fine tone of the wood looking warm in the lamplight.

The Tailor puts on his trousers and shirt and jacket. He passes a comb through his hair. From a drawer in the table under the sheet he takes a tape measure and kneels down before me, stretching the tape along the inside of my leg.

"It's six years since I made a suit," he says.

He drifts like a mist around to my back and then writes the measurements on the wall.

"The shop is the only place good enough for them now," he says.

I watch his brown fingers forming the figures, the strands of hair trailing across his head, his bare ankles going down into his shoes. The shoes have no laces. I look at the tins ranged along the window-ledge, the walls green with damp, the newspapers he lies under at night. He turns then, his breathing like a sleeping dog's, his watery eyes looking into mine, his mouth opening and closing as he tries to find speech.

19

Ma won't stop moving her hands since the funeral. She smooths creases, picks at threads, straightens hair, folds newspapers, polishes spectacles, pokes the fire, ties her laces, adjusts pictures, feeds the dog, shoos hens, opens drawers, tugs at stockings, marks time to aimless tunes. It's

like there's something mechanical inside them that won't let them rest.

"Do you think will Dermot be all right in the town?" she says.

She's on the edge of a wooden chair by the fire. Everyone in the room is looking out the open door seeing nothing. No one answers.

"He's gone to get a new gate for the field with the two cows. I hope he remembers the white thread I asked him for." It's like her head's a crossroads with traffic passing

through. "I told him not to take a drink," she says.

She turns now to me.

"Tell me again about Joe."

I have to tell her how his room was the time I went down to Ipswich to see him, was he thin, the condition of his skin, how much drink he was taking.

"Did you try the police?"

"They wouldn't know."

"The register for people voting?"

"He doesn't vote."

"The hospitals?"

I don't answer her. She drums with her fingers against the wall.

"It was the same way with my Uncle John. The day after the farm went to my father he put some clothes in a bag and went out the door. How could they know then that they'd never see him again? Fine man. They say he had the strength of a dray horse. Everyone came home from England was questioned. Anyone going over would try to have a look. They said prayers. And you know what happened to him. He was found three months after he died in a room in Northampton. They had to put on masks to go into the room. There was a photograph of the island where my grandmother came from on the wall. There wasn't even the money to bring him home to be buried. He was forty-two years in England without a word sent home. It was like he walked into a cloud and vanished." She gets up and reaches for the kettle but then sits down again. "He's one man I'd like to have met," she says.

Dermot's wife can't take any more and she goes into her room and closes the door.

"Couldn't you put an ad in the paper?" she asks me.

She mumbles something that sounds like a prayer.

The next day she stays late in bed and only gets up to see me to the door. She's getting pains in her shoulders, she says. Then she steps back to have a look at me in my new suit. "It's fine work," she says. "I didn't think he had it in him." Outside the sky is low and very dark and the wind is flattening the grass and the smoke as it comes out of the chimney. Anyone in the road is keeping to themselves. All the doors in the townland are closed. "Bad day," Dermot says more than once on the way to the station. I take from my pocket a photograph of Da Matt gave me from the day Da won the prize in Dublin. He's holding his flute out before him. It's like nothing could ever have too much weight in his hands. Matt's eyes are on him and so are the woman's in the cloak and rings. She has one hand raised a little like she wants to ask him something and she's smiling in a way that might please him. Her eyes are lit up and looking only at him. I would like to know what she thinks of him but not what she is trying to ask him because this photograph seems to have no past or future. I hear a cry then, like that of a dog trapped in a hole. There is a smell of fire. We turn a corner in the cart and we're passing above the Tailor's. I can see him in his white underwear taking a lunge at something. He has an axe in his hand and he is moving around before a fire. He lifts the axe and as we move away now I can see what he is doing. He is breaking his loom into pieces and he is throwing the pieces onto the fire.

20

In the beet factory in Ipswich I took the name J. Brady after the name was written in the back of the coat Ma bought me at the Fair. When the paymaster asked me what the J stood for I nearly said Jupiter because I was thinking of P. J. and his desire for a telescope. But I said "Joe" in time. Each Sunday morning after Mass I went to a different

place for a drink but no one had heard of Joe. "What other names did he use?" asked a man from Tipperary.

Working in the beet factory was like sitting inside a wet hayrick on a hot summer's day. There were small windows up by the ceiling where you could see the blue sky and the

presses gave off a fierce heat and steam. You'd be drenched wet working and it seemed you were breathing only steam. I never liked when they put the red beets in a salad, the way they tasted or the stain they left on the plate. There were machines for carting the beets, machines for extracting the sugar and machines for smashing what was left into pulp. I stood stooped over with an open canvas bag waiting for the pulped beet to come rushing down the chute. I filled the bag until it reached a hundredweight, stitched it closed and left it so it could be taken away and fed to cows. I'd rather do the feeding than the filling of bags. It was a short season, but I learned to sew.

When I think of Derbyshire I think of the blue fog in the mornings and the miners walking through it. Why they seemed so lonely I don't know for they were often laughing. They were taking gouges out of the hills the way you'd take off the top of an egg with a knife. We were

putting up screens for the washeries. Black Johnny Fortune was on that job. A tall mournful local man they called Drizzle. The Horse McGurk who played the banjo. And Francie Meehan. He called himself Gallagher after a Donegal hurler and I called myself Rose after one of the men made the flute that was buried with Da. In the digs we were put sleeping in the same bed. He was very long and he always lay on his back and when I woke in the morning the first thing I'd see were his white feet pointing at the ceiling. Sometimes they'd twitch like a fly had landed on them. "Oh those feet," I said to him once. He looked at me like the two of us were out on a mountainside in the rain. "I know," he said. "There's nothing worse than another man's body."

Inside a tent at the Goose Fair in Nottingham I sat on a long bench with Francie and his cousin Martin from Glenties watching a boxer named the Tornado taking a challenge from a black man fighting in his trousers and vest. It was summer and outside the women were all about in their light dresses. But still it was great crack in the tent. For two pounds you got three rounds in the ring with the Tornado and if you beat him you got ten. He had put down a farmer's labourer and a steeplejack but the black man had him foxed. He picked and he opened until the Tornado's arms began to drop. Then he tore into him. The punches were on him like a handful of stones thrown against a wall. He let go with a right to the side of the face then and the Tornado went down, a wave of blood flooding out from his mouth.

"Now," said Francie, turning to me. "Put those arms to

good use. You're the man for it. He's weakened for sure."

We'd had two pints and shorts each before we went in and we'd be going for more after. There was a heat under the tent that made me feel loose and strong. The veins were up in my arms and the blood moving through them. I felt I could lift the ring if I had to. I stood up. Francie and Martin handed me a pound each. I was thinking of the way Da filled a sack with sand and showed Joe and me how to get the power into our punches with our legs. I held up my hand with the banknotes and went up into the ring. I thought I could be like John Joe was in the train and

frighten the Tornado with the size of my arms but when I
handed over the money and was introduced he looked me in
the eye and winked. We stood facing each other. I led with
my left and was looking to bury the right into the centre of
his gut. I threw six punches and he pushed them all away.
He was like a man clearing slow-moving bees that were
annoying him on a summer's day. He bounced two jabs off
my forehead and threw a right in under my eye. It was like
having logs land on you from the sky. He got me under the
arms then and pushed me against the ropes.

"Where are you from, boy?" he said. I told him. "Didn't I know it? I'm only two parishes away. Now go down easy when I hit you and we can go for a pint."

"The last man beat you and so will I," I said. I was thinking of the ten pounds and the way Francie and Martin would be looking at me. I pushed him away.

"Don't you know the two of us are partners?" he said.

"Some partner that opened a hole in your mouth," I said.

"Whenever we fight we keep a small balloon filled with dyed water in our mouths," said the Tornado. He seemed to be pleading with me. I moved in on him and threw a right that flew a foot clear of his head.

"Have you a wife and family?" he said.

"No."

"Isn't it truly pitiful the things I have to do?"

I took a jab on the top lip, he crouched low like he was going to bring his right up all the way from the floor and then he hit me with a straight left I never saw square on the point of the chin. I went down like a crow shot from the sky. It's strange how it doesn't hurt when you get hit clean.

I don't remember the name I used in Nottingham. We had a good night in the bar after the Goose Fair, the black man telling us all about sparring with Sugar Ray Robinson in America. We were working on a road that time, me on one side of the tamper levelling the concrete, Francie on the other. We had plenty of money even after sending some home and we drank it all. Cleary I think it was I called myself, after a priest.

In Kent we had the job of destroying air raid shelters.

They were the devil, some of them, with steel running through the walls and roof. Francie got hit with a lump of concrete flew off the end of the jackhammer. The blood ran down over his eye and he looked at me like the world should be ready to mourn him, but I told him it wasn't half the blow I got from the Tornado at the Goose Fair when he threw me into the ring, and he stayed quiet then. The orchards were lovely to walk past on a Sunday, the scent of apples. There was a girl there. Margaret Bracewell. She worked in a shop selling newspapers and sweets. I stopped in the evening and stayed sometimes for an hour. She lived with nuns in Dorset through the war because of the bombing and they were very kind to her, she said. They taught her all about working with lace and in the time she was there, she said, she made an altar cloth. She had lovely small hands. We went walking one Sunday along lanes and over hills and past orchards smelling of apples talking all the time, but when we got to the gate where she lived I had more thoughts running in my head than I could account for in my mouth and I stood in the road and said nothing. I remember the way she sighed. I remember the way she shrugged her shoulders and walked up the path to her door. Her cheeks were like the apples. In Kent I took the name Patterson, after a town in America where relations of Ma's lived.

In Bedford I was slab laying. In Coventry it was drainage pipes. There was a site in Barnet must have been four acres anyway and there it was mostly shuttering. I carried the hod for a week in Blackheath but I hadn't the balance. McNamara was a name I used, after the song sung by

Americans. O'Neill for the great king of the North. Loss, because of the bandleader. You could be on a site those days and half of them would be calling themselves Michael Collins for the crack. I was underpinning with Francie in Chelsea. He'd be down on his knees in the dirt those days, singing.

> In Liffey Street had furniture with fleas and bugs I sold it,
> And at the Bank a big placard I often stood to hold it.

In New Street I sold hay and straw and
    in Spitalfields made bacon.
In Fishamble Street was at the grand old trade of
    basket making.

He called himself Nasser to annoy the English paymaster and I was Wilson after the young boy was learning the flute from Da. It felt strange with that on me but I thought I would give it a try. Francie and me walking up the Kilburn High Road ahead of two men. "They're from Clare," said Francie to me out of the side of his mouth. "You can tell by the way they whistle." They had ten years on us maybe. "You'll not go home again boys," called out the one with the black straw hat sitting on the back of his head, and the two of them laughed. We had digs in Cavendish Road with a landlady named Chandler. I won't stop to think about her now. She gave us a plateful of eggs and rashers and black pudding that Sunday morning and we went straight up the road to Cricklewood in the sunlight without stopping for Mass and then into the Crown for the opening at noon. It was the day of the All-Ireland and bets were being laid and pints were flying. I left the accordion in the digs but a lad from Kerry gave me the loan of his and I played them "The Golden Castle". We bought bottles of stout over the bar and made for Alexandra Palace with our radios, Francie, Martin, myself and another cousin of theirs, a pale little fellow called Ivan who was never before out of his own parish. All his life he'd tended sheep in the hills with his father. At Archway we stood on the pavement waiting to cross but he was trembling.

"The speed of the cars!" he said. He had a drowning man's grip on Martin's arm. A bus stopped and when it went off again we were left in a cloud of grey smoke. "Oh Martin," I heard Ivan say. "The bus!" I could only barely make out his shape. He bent over then and left the whole of his breakfast in the road before us. I could see the yellow from the yolk of the egg he'd eaten running through the rest of it. "The bus," he said. "I wouldn't mind," said Francie, "but he only drank minerals in the Crown." When we got to Alexandra Palace the crest of the hill was crowded with Irishmen tuning their

radios to get the signal from home. We drank the stout and listened to the wild calls from the hillside as the points were scored and afterwards with the sun still pouring down on us we played twenty-fives. That was the day of the All-Ireland and I won four pounds at the cards. "Did you know they have a statue here of Oliver Cromwell?" said Francie. "I saw it myself." We were making for Kilburn in the top of a bus. Ivan had a handkerchief in his hand made into a pouch with a length of red string. He untied it and held it out to me, a smile on him that showed all his teeth. "Earth from Donegal," he said. "He wanted to be a priest," said Martin. That was meant to explain it. "But he doesn't drink enough!" said Francie and we all laughed, even Ivan. We had plates of boiled bacon and then made for the Old Bell. A small round man with an angry face under his hat came towards us with a baby's pushchair out in front of him. There was a box on the seat and he was blowing on a mouth organ to clear a path. Anybody didn't move fast enough he cursed them. I thought of Baby and how Da always greeted her and it caught me. We had pints in the Old Bell and pints in the Volunteer and pints in the Black Lion. That was the day of the All-Ireland and the day I had luck with me for it was the first time I ever saw Maggie Doyle. She had a dress on the colour of sand and red shoes and she was walking across the room like a cloud was carrying her, leaning a little forward, the red hair falling across her left eye, her face set, the mouth open a little, then the smile breaking first in the lines around her mouth and then up into her eyes until her whole face was alight when she sat next to a woman wearing a broad straw hat. I remember not only the way she looked when she came into the bar but the way it felt the moment before, the smoke rising from the cigarettes, the young boy selling papers, the Sligo man in the grey suit with his fiddle case across his knees and his finger tapping at the side of his brow. Francie imploring Ivan to take a short. Then Maggie and as I remember it everything around her blurs. I think she looks over at me once from her chair but maybe not. I have the accordion with me and when I play "Come West Along the Road" the Horse McGurk gets up, takes off his shirt and vest and dances around the tables with a chair between his teeth. I think of the way the lines break around her mouth when she starts to smile, the alertness of the brain behind it. "That was fine playing," she says to me as she goes. She is looking over her shoulder as she walks away. The day of the All-Ireland. Maybe she's been thinking of saying it since she first heard the tune.

21

When the landlady's door is open it's a sign for Francie that the husband is away at the bus depot and for him to come in. She started him at it the second week we were there and ever after when he saw the crack in the door he made for the stairs like a greyhound. I never got a look inside. "What's it like in there?" I asked him. "It's all pink," he said, like it was a great wonder.

She barred him once for two weeks when she got mad at him about the smoke. I came into the room from the bath with my hair slicked down and the Tailor's suit on me for it was Wednesday and I was going to the Bamba dance. Francie was in a chair with his feet up on the bed and the *Donegal Democrat* spread across his lap. A pig's head was boiling away in the pot on the gas ring. He was in his work clothes still and his eyes were flickering. "Mind you don't fall asleep," I said to him as I left. Maggie wasn't at the dance, I remember that. I kept a watch on the door. When I got back to Cavendish Road and went into the room there was Francie stretched across the bed snoring, the paper over his face and smoke thick as a mountain mist filling the room, the pot and the pig's head that was in it both as black as a boot. Mrs Chandler looked at us hard the next morning at breakfast like she was thinking what sentence she would impose on us, the sentence of exile maybe, but she denied him his rations instead.

I met him one morning on the stairs carrying his shoes. He looked like a rumpled sheet. "She only gave me an hour's sleep," he said. "Every time I dropped off she was at me. It's worse than digging trenches in the rain." We were laying railway lines that time and it was heavy work. When the green-eyed cat came into the room and leapt onto Francie he drop-kicked it straight through the open window. He

could be in bad humour if he didn't get his sleep. Wherever the cat went it must have passed the kitchen window for straight away Mrs Chandler was in the room in her apron throwing our clothes down the stairs. We headed down the Kilburn High Road. "You can ride the landlady," said Francie. "But don't blackguard the cat."

22

When Francie is away laying the gas lines in Portsmouth I get very lonely in the room. We're in a basement that time in Quex Road. The room has one picture in a blue wooden frame of a blond boy milking a cow and it makes it worse. The room gets no light. In the week I take a few pints in the Old Bell and make my way back to Quex Road eating something out of a newspaper. One night at closing time I'm walking behind a red-haired man with mud on his boots, the trousers falling off him, the paper rolled up in his jacket pocket and him taking the two sides of the pavement from all the drink and I know it is me. I know it is all of us. On Sunday it's Mass and the Crown and after two o'clock it's murder. I lean on the railings smoking cigarettes I don't like. I read the paper and fail to reach the end of a story. I put on the radio but the words get lost. We have a clock and I look at it. The minutes go by like water dripping from a tap. Some time around six the walls seem to move in on me.

I know that something bad is going to happen.

On the top floor is a man from Belfast always wears a suit and a tie. It's dark under his eyes and dark in them too so you can't find him, like a cellar with the only light falling through a small dirty window. He has manners like an usher at church. He lifts the hat up off his head whenever he greets you. He's an actor, he says, Albert Maskey of the Ormeau Road, Belfast. I don't know how he does it for he's afflicted with a stutter whenever he tries to explain something complicated. I see him through the dust and the grey

light of the stairwell leaving out a saucer of milk for the cat. Whenever he's not busy with something else he's cleaning and filing his nails. "Good grooming is essential for an actor," he says. The right brow travels up the forehead after he says something like that, like what he says surprises him.

He likes to take a glass of scotch at six every evening and somehow it's come about that I go up to him on Thursdays. I never saw the bed unmade or even with a dent in the cover. Socks and jumpers folded along a shelf. A glass cabinet for the drink. A cup and saucer with a teapot on the table ready for the morning. In the corner is a little bottle with the top off filled with green liquid to give off the smell of trees. You'd think it was the room of a man would drive a car for a bishop only for the pictures of women in frames along the shelf above his bed. Beside them is a crown made from plaster and painted gold. Had he worn it on the stage? "Not yet," he tells me, the eyes dark shadows.

I ask him about the women.

"I've known them all, you know," he says. He laughs, but the laugh fades away like the bark of a tired dog. He gets up from his chair and puts on his spectacles. Each one he gives a name. Rita, Eustace, Marie-Thérèse, Lucy. Did he get them from *The Lives of the Saints*? There's one he calls Princess with black hair looks like she's been surprised and likes it. Their teeth have a kind of shining white like you'd see in a star. They have bands in their hair, some of them, and you can see the lines of their bodies because of the tightness of their clothes. One is dressed in a long gown, gold and white, that reaches to the floor, her blonde hair piled up and trailing down her neck, diamonds on her ears. He tells me the story of each romance as he gives them their names. The one he worked with on the cruise out of Barcelona. The one from Dublin was going to be a nun. The one played Cleopatra in Derby he stole from another actor. The one from Greenland he met looking at tombs in the museum. Places like Lisbon, Istanbul and Tangier come into it somehow. "I've been busy, I've travelled," he says. "I've loved them all." Again the fading laugh that you can't believe.

Francie comes back from the work in Portsmouth and I get a little steadier. We get a meal every evening at the café. We change our shoes before going for a drink. We get through Sunday with cards or a long walk.

When something is going to happen you can get a warning. Like when the room kept moving but I went still just before Maggie walked into the bar. I sit up in the bed that night like someone's blown a whistle into my ear. I ease back down onto the pillow but I'm a long way from sleep. It's ten past two on the clock. There's a breeze outside and the shadows of the trees in the garden move across the picture of the boy with the cow. I am in the bed by the window and Francie is over by the wall. I see his back go up and down with the rhythm of sleep. What can I do while I'm waiting? I try to think my way through all the notes of "The Green-Crowned Lass". There's a noise then, something moving through branches, the splintering of wood, and then a crash like a load of boards hitting the ground from a snapped cable. There's a slow dying moan and then the silence, more still than before. I cannot hear the breeze. I draw back the curtain. On the ground facing me are the wide dark eyes of Albert Maskey. The top of his head is caved in a little on the side where he landed and his broken arm is stretched across his chest and shoulder, the hand up and open like he's asking for something. There's dirt in his mouth. He's a suit and tie on, everything in place, and he's wearing the gold crown was up on the shelf above his bed.

I couldn't get to the bottom of it.

The night he told me about the girls I looked at their pictures before I left the room. The way they posed, a hand on the hip, a look over the shoulder. The paper was thin and the edges of some were uneven. He'd cut them from magazines and put them in frames.

That was bad what happened to Albert Maskey, but it wasn't the thing I was fearing somehow when the walls were moving in.

23

To get to the graveyard you must walk across sand. It is a ring of earth and grass and stone cleansed by the sea wind set in the water and connected to the shore at Baby's house by the neck of sand. There was rain in the afternoon after Da buried the mare but now there is light. In the evening light the green of the grass deepens, a stitching of silver can be seen in the rocks, gold spreads and dives and sparkles on the water and the shadows of the gravestones are long. All the things are there on the graves. The shoes of children, jumpers half knit, flowers, coins, photographs, a mouth organ and a flat cap. There is a message on paper rolled into the neck of a bottle of stout. The gravedigger with the blond hair and the lower teeth which come up over his lip is moving along with a broom sweeping where he can. "Taking the bad luck off the graves," he says again and again.

On the grave of the mare there is nothing only clods of

mud from the afternoon rain. Da says after he's shot her and put an end to the desperate noise she was making that he means to cut a piece from the tail of her colt and leave it on the grave. I am sitting on the wall watching the sun go down over the graveyard. Matt was there leaving a saucer with blackberries on it on the grave of his wife but now he and the gravedigger are both gone. The shadows lose their edge and fade away as the sun drops. To bury a horse you need a grave twice the length and twice the width of a man's. I hear then the sound of crying, a gagged and pitiful sound. I can't

find it but I know it is coming from the earth. It falls away from the effort and then rises, a wild complaint. I know this sound. It is the sound of the mare in her sickness. I see then the mud of her grave begin to move, churning, restless, the clods of mud breaking and falling from a struggle below. I can feel the force of it as I grip the stones of the wall, a force greater than the weight of the earth upon it. A hoof breaks through, pawing at the air, a kind of caress. Then the two forelegs, smeared with mud. They thrash and kick, the two hooves embed deep in the mud, there is a surge of halted

power from under the earth, and another, and then with a great heave the horse is finally up, wet and stained, the mud falling away, blood still seeping from the wound in the side of her head where Da shot her. She shakes the grave from her and she arches her neck. Then she fixes me with her eye.

Christ. It's nearly four o'clock. I feel like I've walked off the edge of a scaffold in the dark. The heart is pounding. I hear the footsteps of the girl who lives below me climbing the stairs. She has trouble getting the key in the lock. The drink, I suppose, and why not? A night bus passes outside. Lonely sounds. This is the bed where Maggie remembered her dreams. She could tell you every twist of them. I don't want dreams now. There's none I have that don't cause me bother somehow. Where did I get a horse like that?

The graveyard. Mrs Carney tells me her husband is sick and I'll have to look after the making of the grave myself. She goes into a shed and comes back out with a spade and hands it me. Dermot's been drinking whiskey since the day Ma died and it falls to me. "Where am I to dig?" I ask her. "You'll take up your father's coffin and make the grave deep enough for the two of them." She goes back in and closes the door. I look at this door, its red blistering paint, the brass door knocker with their name on it sent by the daughter in Scotland probably. Why couldn't they even get the paint on right? Why isn't he fit to dig a grave? I would like to take the spade and drive it through the heart of the door.

The month of my mother's death is November. Dark clouds rolling into the hillside as I walk with Carney's spade across the neck of sand to the graveyard. "They opened her up and the cancer was everywhere," said Dermot's wife. "She was black with it. It was a mercy she went." I find Da's grave and begin to dig. In the earth there's splintered wood, a button from a woman's dress, nails, shells dropped by gulls, a shard of blue delft, a coffee can from America. They opened her up and she was black inside. How much of this can I bear? I dig. Everything is shaking. I dig until I come to Da. The force of the air seems enough to break my bones. I dig around the coffin and I haul it up. Don't spill out, I beg him. It begins to rain. I get back in the grave to dig some more. I kneel. I ask for help, help from anywhere. When the grave is deep enough I try to get out but I slip in the mud. I grab at clumps of grass and the edges of the gravestones, I pull myself up and I edge the coffin closer to the mouth of the grave. I lie in the mud and guide it down. Please God the wood will hold. I hear him rolling inside. I get the coffin to the base of the grave, I right it and I cover it with grass. What is this thing that is on me? I remember anger from when the paymaster in Blackheath wouldn't pay me what was owed. I remember Kate Creevy boarding the train. I remember loneliness and the walls of Quex Road. I remember pure sadness. This is not any of those but some of all of them maybe and more. What is the more, though? I see myself running around the graveyard, up over the wall and into the sea. There would be no comfort in sleep or in drink. It is like something is covering me that threatens my breath. It is like something is moving that will break things inside me.

When I get to London I find that I cannot understand the bricks. The train passes through tunnels and cuttings

and past buildings all of them made of bricks the colour of dried blood. The bricks make up the walls and the hard pitted clay makes up the bricks. I think of all the bricks and all the little holes, some the size of pinpricks only. How can there be so many bricks? How can there be so much time to place them into rows? When I lie in bed in Quex Road I think of a building and I think of how many bricks it takes to make up its width. I go upwards from the base and count the rows. I think of the lack of bricks in the doors and the windows and where the building ends for it cannot go through the sky and I try to find the number of bricks in the wall that is facing me as I picture it. There are the front and back of the building and maybe the two sides and still more sides maybe, there are bricks in the inside walls, bricks under the ground, bricks that form roads, bricks in sewers. Bricks in the buildings when I turn out the door, bricks up and down the Kilburn High Road and bricks forever out into the world.

There are bricks from all the years that make up the walls. When I pass them I try to think of the men who put them there. Who told them where to place the bricks? What way did they shave? What was the drink they liked the best? I fall in among them and among the ages of the city.

The Horse McGurk is driving the crane. You'd think he was throwing the hammer the way he swings the load of bricks. We're building flats in Spitalfields. He's leaving the pallets of bricks down at intervals along the wall. The banksman has given up guiding him for he knows the Horse will pay him no heed. He's moving closer to where the wall turns and he'll need to get the pallet in under the scaffolding, the loads swinging and crashing to the ground. I think what it would be like to ride the pallet into the wall. The banksman is smoking a cigarette. All the weight of the bricks swinging at the end of the cable. If he misses the gap the load will smash into a wall or the scaffold. He swings the arm of the crane a little to get the rhythm going. I think of how the bricks will smash into powder and clay. He makes a pass and then pulls back because he's going to miss.

The load begins to swing again. I am seeking the darkness. The load goes back a final time and I leap onto it. Everything in me pulls towards the earth as the load swings down. I begin to feel the great power of the crash before it happens. I see it might move towards the side wall and I try to guide it there with my weight. The powder of the bricks and blood and bone and darkness. The wall gets closer. I can see the holes in the bricks. I wait.

The touch of the Horse is sure. He lets me gently down to the ground.

24

The door is not green. There's no priest nor porter nor songs inside. The door is iron and it is open. Inside there is fire.

What I could do then. I could forget my name. I could lie in bed for a week. I could seek the darkness. I could hunch my shoulders, grin like a fool and say, Any chance of a start? I could go to the wrong door. I could frighten Francie. I could lose the music. I could pass like a ghost through the city, the city itself ghostly. I could walk without knowing it.

I can see the boy standing on his brother's back painting the door with his hands. If I try to follow him through potato fields and sites and rooms to the place where everything was burning I get lost. I remember the poison and shame and heat. I remember waiting for the peace that would not come.

There is smoke in the bar and the tall windows let in the evening light. It must be summer, the way the light is, the way people sit in their shirts before their drinks. I am drinking gin because I never had it before. I do not know this place nor how I got to it. A radio is playing. There is a ukulele and a woman singing about the seashore. I picture her fat and blonde, the hair turning up at the ends rigid as wire. I picture the red lipstick. She sounds cheerful and cruel and I want all this to go away. There are men studying formsheets and men looking through the smoke to the light of the window. Alone at the bar, sitting on a stool, is a man with skin the colour of mahogany nearly, his hands clutching the sides of his head. I drink down the gin and go to the bar for another. I look at the man as I wait, at the creases in the skin of his neck. He is from Pakistan maybe, or Bangladesh. He is looking into his beer and his lips are moving and he is speaking. He is moving back and forth according to the pattern of what he is saying. I can't make it out. I wonder is he praying. I wonder are we the same. I bend lower to hear what he is saying and he feels me there. He looks up. His eyes are yellow and brown and red. "I wish God would destroy the world," he says.

25

I've finished the tea and swallowed the pills the nurse brought me in the little paper cup. She stretches up in her white uniform to draw the curtain and tells us all that we should go to sleep. The new man beside me does as he is told and the old boy across is asleep already. It is two-thirty on a Monday afternoon. I have clean pyjamas, clean sheets and a clean face. I am sitting up in the bed with my hands folded across my lap and my eyes wide open staring at a spot on the wall opposite. I'm awake like I've had a bucket of sea water thrown over me.

Into the room, carrying a box of chocolates, steps my

mother's Uncle John. He makes straight for me and sits down at the end of my bed. I don't know how I built him the way I did but he is a fine man, a lean islander's face, the blue eyes full of sea and sky, the lines around his eyes and mouth receiving his laughter. What way was he when the men in masks found him in the room in Northampton? He has a jacket on Roscoe would have liked and a gold ring. The flat cap is new and sits on his knee. There are men on the Kilburn High Road you can only see unfinished buildings in their eyes. You cannot see the city in his face. You see

the sea. You see him with his hand on the till of a boat cutting through water. He looks right just the way the house does when I think of it set into the side of the green hill in Labasheeda. But while the lines smile his mouth can't, for a scar curves like a turning centipede from the left corner of his nose, down onto his lip and into his mouth. This part of him cannot move.

"When I first left I lived in New York," he says. "I found a patch of grass in among the buildings and the concrete and on Sundays I would go there and sit in it. It was just like the grass on the rise of Tullaherin." He laughs and gives my leg a squeeze through the covers like I know all about the bitterness of this joke.

He starts with the two houses on Tullaherin and moves in a sweep across the townland. He tells me the colours of the doors the day he left. He tells me what fields had the finest animals. He tells me about him who could throw heavy stones the furthest, made the best thatch, could ride a horse standing on its back, lift and carry a curragh on his own, shout loudest, sing sweetest, drink deepest, charm women. He told me about her that reared children that could run fast, had the loveliest hair, moved with the lightest step, said words in French, argued with the priest, remembered the generations, made the sweetest butter.

"I read a book once," he says. "I read many one time. The thing about a book is that the man who is writing it brings all the lives from all the different places and makes them flow together in the same stream. As they move down towards the end it's like they have loops and holes and shapes that all fit together just nicely so that they're just one big piece really. You can look back and see how all of them got where they are. That's the time the writer brings the book to an end and there's no seeing past it. I'd like to meet the man who wrote a book like that so I could ask him where he got those lives. I never met anything like that in all my time. I look back and I see a big field full of mud, people and animals sliding and me sliding with them. There's no end. There's just times when some are standing and some are fallen."

He tells me then he's heard about the music I make with

the accordion and I want so badly to play for him to keep him there. He fades in and out like a radio losing its signal.

He leaves the chocolates down beside the bed, and he stands up. He places his large warm hand on my brow and makes a cross like a priest giving ashes before Lent. "Those people from home, any that remember me tell them I was asking. We're the same, you and me. Tell them we forgive them and they should forgive us."

He goes then, the bitter laugh he means for me breaking and falling behind him like a ring of smoke.

26

The spade feels heavy in my hand. On the scaffolding I fear a fall. When there's crack I step away with shame at the way the words are so slow and broken in my mouth. The accordion is the worst. It has so many buttons and I cannot find or remember them all.

They have me sweeping. I sweep dust and shavings of wood and food that falls to the ground. When I am doing this work I have in my mind only the picture of myself with the broom in my hand. I could stuff a saddle. From this there is no hiding.

I wait with the others in the early morning darkness along the railings in Camden Town. They are all in their coats leaning over, smoking cigarettes. Men who would live in your ear in a bar hold back from speech. They look serious. They look like they could be looking down into a river watching a swimming race. We wait for the Animal to come and pick the gang. When he steps down from the van he will take his coat off even in winter for he wants everyone there to see his arms. From the back he looks like a turf stack and from the front he's a fright. He's a scar like a trench running down from his eye, the eyes two halfpennies. In the centre is the nose. It's like a big potato breaking up through the ground. It bends one way, then another and then back as it goes from the bridge to the tip. Many's the man waiting on the railings

would like to be the man who broke it for him. The mouth curves around his face like a dog's. You have to watch him. You could be talking with him in a bar in a peaceful way about greyhounds or the price of drink and he'd rear up on you. He could break the pint glass on the edge of the table and bring it right up to your eye. When he walks his hands face backwards. His right arm swings like a weight at the end of a chain. Men from Connemara inspired by their hatred took him into the toilet in the Spotted Dog in Willesden and broke it over a knee.

I wait there mornings for work with Francie and Martin and the others. Most always I get it even if it's only sweeping. Ivan came with us when we first went down, a scarf and woollen hat on him and the donkey jacket so big he was like a clothes peg holding up a tent. When the Animal stepped from the van and saw him he knew he could have sport. "And what can you do, man of straw?" he said. The voice would just cut you. "I can dig," says Ivan. "You couldn't dig the shite from your own arse," says the Animal. He leans over with the two hands on his knees and lets out a roar. Anyone he spots not laughing doesn't work that day. "I'm going to work on the buses," says Ivan to us.

I sit alone in the room with the accordion and try to get the feel of it. I lift it up and down like you would a baby to try to get the right sense of its weight. I move my fingers over the buttons. I play tunes Da tried to teach Joe when he was a child. On a Saturday afternoon with Francie at the bookie's I sit on the edge of the bed and I try to play "She Moves Through the Fair". My finger slips from a button and I get a flat sound like the call of a goose. I start again. The notes which are so full of this yearning hold just right until they move and fade into those that follow. I know then that you play not for what you can give anyone or for what they will think of you but only for the sake of the tune itself. It goes to the point where it seems it can get away from me but doesn't. I can hold it in. I hold it as though in a dance. This is the time when no one can touch you. I am just like this when I hear Francie. "Jesus Christ, will you ever stop?" he says. He's standing in the centre of the room with a look on him like a thirsty man begging for coins in the street. "The sadness of it," he says, and he goes back out.

27

The window fills with the face of the King. The hut is by the side of the road in Kennington and the glass is smeared with rainwater and coal dust and the fumes from buses but still I can see the long heavy jaw and the small round ears sticking out from the side of his head like bottle tops. I am drinking tea. The King raps lightly on the window. The hand itself is like a turfcutter's loy. "You'll not take tea without permission from the King," he says. I'd heard of the King in Coventry, I'd heard of him in Luton and I'd heard of him all around London. Now he is before me.

I go out to greet him. He reaches out the hand and I take it. He puts his face up close to mine and I can see the long lines and the scar on his neck from where a strut broke when he was tunnelling and the wall fell in on him. "I've been in every bar in Camden and Kilburn and Cricklewood looking for the man can play me 'The Mason's Apron'. I was in Glasgow and they didn't know it there either. Would you be the man for me now?"

I tell him I can play the tune and he rolls us each a cigarette and we lean back against the wall of the hut to smoke them. The green van pulls up and the Animal gets in, the springs going down under his weight. "Ever since I met that creature I've hated the people of Louth," says the King.

Two lads in their vests studying the trade of bricklaying heave a bag of cement off the back of a lorry and drag it along the ground. If it hits a bit of glass or the point of a stick it will open up onto the road. They come to a low wall then and try to lift it to the other side. But they can't get hold of it. It slips from their hands. They both reach down at the same time to grip it underneath and their two heads meet with a thump just over the nose. "Will you look at them?" says the King. He leaves the cigarette on the ledge of the window and walks over. He tells the lads to stand aside. He leans over from the waist, grips the bag with his teeth and lifts it over the wall. He walks back to me then and takes up the cigarette. "The thing about that beast the Animal," says the King, "is that he's a coward." Everyone mixing muck, everyone in the trench, everyone hauling bricks or pipes, people passing on the pavement, they're all looking at him. Francie told me about the time he saw the King working the jackhammer when a woman came up to him and asked the way to the post office. "That way, madam," he said, lifting the hammer with the one arm and pointing the way.

They say no man alive could dig like the King. He dug up wooden water mains, unknown tunnels, ancient walls and bones. He saw the timbering go and a tunnel turn into a grave. He'd go right under a road on his own lit by a candle, emptying his own load with a tin bucket. I saw him past the time of the fullness of his strength but still I saw him lift the bag of cement with his teeth that day in Kennington. Then later I saw the paleness come into his features and the knees begin to weaken and I heard the rattling down in his lungs from his days under the ground digging the wet clay. Then came the time when no one could tell you where he was. If you asked anyone about him they would tell you a story of the wonder of his strength but they had not seen nor heard of him. He moved into the past.

I thought of him on a day when the train from Leyton stalled on the tracks over the graveyard. It was winter, black low clouds rolling like waves in a heavy sea, the wind troubling the long grass. There was no one in the graveyard save for the one funeral just below me. The undertaker holding onto his tall hat in the wind, the pallbearers he'd hired shouldering the coffin, the priest reading from his book, the words scattering. No wife, no children, no neighbours, just one man in a trench coat, his hair white and blowing around his head in the circling wind. This was the place in the graveyard without stones or flowers, the common grave for those who are poor or who have no name or who leave no mark. The coffin is made of planks of pine. The lights in the train fall on the faces of the passengers. They read or they stare out ahead of them or they look into the distance. There are none that look down at the funeral. There are none that register the attentiveness of the man with the trench coat and white hair. I cannot think of who it is he is mourning. I think instead of the King. There were none who knew him who did not feel the power of the King. He bore it lightly, and in this way you felt strength when you were with him. If this were his funeral, I do not know of a name they could call him.

28

Francie is before the microphone with a pint in his hand and the other arm reaching out while he sings "I'll Take You Home Again, Kathleen" like John McCormack. Everyone in the Mother Redcap thinks it's great crack except the American, who is bent over his recording machine turning the dials. When he's everything right with the machine he asks Francie to sit down and the Clareman to go up with his fiddle. It's Sunday afternoon past closing time but they're still pouring pints for the American's paying. We're there to hear the Clareman and because there's nothing else to do on a Sunday afternoon.

The Clareman is a fine player, I think, very gentle with the bow. He takes the drive out of a tune with the light way he has of playing, but he gives you the sweetness. He can get the tune inside you that way. I sit in with him for "The Star Above the Garter" and we go along nicely. The American gives me five pounds and sends over another pint. Between tunes he's very busy with his arms like a policeman directing traffic. And he's as loud as he is big. When he settles back down to his machine and the Clareman begins to play Maggie comes over and sits down beside me. What had we together by then? We'd had three dances at the Pride of Erin and a walk along the canal one Sunday when I saw her by accident. The Clareman plays "Spailpín a Rún" and I never heard it better. Just the way he gets hold of the tune makes me want to play. Maggie leans over, her hand on my

knee. She's easy that way, like a girl in the country. "I heard you had to go to the hospital with burns," she says. She pushes her red hair up with her two hands and lets it fall over the left eye. The other is looking at me, brown and warm and clear. You cannot look at this eye and lie. "I got burned trying to crawl into the back of the television in the Archway Tavern," I tell her. Her right hand goes up and I think it will go to my face but she thinks better of it maybe and it falls onto my shoulder and down my arm. "I know about that," she says. "But you're all right now." Her touch is light like a small breeze and I remember the weight and the distance of it and I remember the way it sent a current up my spine and through my head. I can get it now as I think of it, very light and warm but with the power to lift me clear of the earth.

29

When the priest calls the last of the numbers and Con Hogan from Belmullet finds he's won nothing he tears his raffle tickets into small pieces and throws them into the air. They fall back down into his hair and onto his shoulders and legs. The Woodbine is burning low in his fingers, the smoke rising up through the curls of his hair and around the shreds of the tickets. "Everyone was together then. On bicycles," he says. This was a speech which he started in his brain before speaking. "You could see who they

were. Now they're all in motor cars. How can you see who anyone is in a motor car?" He draws on the Woodbine and doesn't notice how it's burning his finger. His legs are crossed and he's leaned way over to one side and I wonder will he fall from his chair.

"Do you see that man there?" says the King. He's a bottle of John Powers with him and he places it on the table before sitting down. There's himself, me, Francie, Martin, Maggie and her cousin Helen Maguire just over from Tyrone. I feel about him sitting down with us the way I felt about walking up the town on the Fair Day with Joe Brennan the time I was hired by Casey. "Just after he arrived from Belmullet I went with him to the pictures. 'Hold on,' he says as we're on the way, and he goes into a shop with me following. 'I'd like twenty-four Mars bars,' he says to the girl behind the counter. She looks over to me. 'Is he all right?' she says. 'Why?' says I. 'He's asked me for twenty-four Mars bars.' 'Give them to him,' says I. When we went into the street I looked at him hard and I said to him, 'You'll make a show of me.' I had two and he had twenty-two. That's Con Hogan from Belmullet."

The Animal walks into the church hall, a man to either side of him in case anyone would have a go at him. One was from Newcastle, I remember, and the other from Louth. They sit down under a picture from the African missions. There's a nun opening bottles behind the bar and another handing out plates of sandwiches. We all take a sandwich when she comes to us and when there's just one on the plate the King leans over to me and says, "Hold on to that one for me until I get back." He goes right out the door and when he comes back again he calls out to the Animal, "Here you are, John," he says. "Don't go hungry," and the Animal takes the last sandwich. "You'll see something now," says the King to me. The Animal takes a gouge the size of a fist from the sandwich, the jaws working under the red nose. He stops then, bread falling from his open mouth, the little black eyes as wide as they'll go. "Christ Jesus," he says to the man from Louth, "I thought the priest bought his meat from Corrigan's," and he spits what's left in his mouth onto the floor.

"What did you give him?" I say to the King.

"A rare thing to find in a church hall," he says.

"What would that be?"

He leans over close then so the women won't hear. "A condom filled with raw sewage."

"Holy Mary," says Francie. "He'd break a man's back for less."

"Do you know what's almost as bad as a man from Louth?" asks the King. "A man would take a job in a factory or on trains."

The Animal comes over to wash the taste of sewage from his mouth with a glass of the King's whiskey. "God save all here," he says with a kind of smirk. "Do you know what that bollocks of a works inspector from the council got me out on a Sunday evening for?" he says. He swallows down the glass of whiskey. "One fucking inch. 'That trench,' he says, 'is an inch further out into the road than is shown on the plans. You'll have to fill it in and dig again.' Can you credit it? A fucking inch. I'll fill him in before I'll fill in the hole."

You can only see how truly ugly the Animal is from up close, the head narrowing up nearly to a point from the shoulders. The lips look like they're filled with water, the huge nose like something half eaten by a dog. He'd talk like that in front of your grandmother. "What's a fucking inch?" he demands of the table.

Maggie with a serious look like she's working through a mathematical problem raises her finger in the air and says, "An inch is a lot on a nose."

The Animal becomes suddenly still and numb like a stunned bullock in an abattoir. The King's shoulders are shaking as he pours himself another glass of whiskey. Martin looks like he'll explode, Francie like he's found a five-pound note on the road.

Maggie's not moving, but I think there's a smile forming within her. She saw an opening and she moved in, her mind a blade. From that day I could never turn away from her.

30

In the picture a young girl in a red and white dress is planting flowers in a window-box outside her room. Every day that hot summer week while we dig up the pavement beneath her window in Ladbroke Grove we can look up and see her. By the Friday she knows each of our names. There's Myles Walsh, Pat Kennedy and the Iroquois from Glasgow. John Conneely from Connemara is sitting against the wall eating an apple when the girl from the window comes down and gives him a wooden chair. John was sixty-three that time and anyone could see the knees were bad. Francie has his foot up on a low wall and is drinking milk from a pint bottle. He is bothered for a moment by a bee and when he puts the bottle back up to his mouth a black man with a straw hat and a blue and white striped suit walks past, gold rings shining on his fingers and a cigarette in its holder gripped between his teeth. He is wearing the finest white shirt I ever saw.

We're talking about the Animal.

"He's no gentleman," says John. "He put a lit cigarette up into the arse of a cat. A gentleman would never do a thing like that."

"You're right there," says Myles.

Francie leaves the milk bottle down and lifts the jack-hammer.

"Martin was digging in a hole under the Marylebone

Road on Monday when he hit something hard with the spade. 'What's that?' he says to himself and cleans away the clay. The thing is big and dark and it has writing on it. It's made of lead. 'What do you make of that?' he says to Jack O'Rourke, who's beside him in the hole. Jack puts the glasses on and takes a look. He's a great reader of books as you know. He looks all around it like it's something he might buy. Finally he gives the verdict. 'A Roman coffin,' he says, putting the glasses back into his pocket. Martin crawls out of the hole and phones Muldoon over in the yard. But he can only get the Crow. 'The Animal is taking his lunch over in the Princess Louise,' says the Crow. So Martin phones over to the bar and gets the Animal on the line and explains to him all about the Roman coffin. There's a pause then while he thinks about it. Then he says, 'Break the fucking thing up and bury it.' He didn't want anyone from a museum holding up the job. That's the Animal, the friend of art and science."

He puts the tip of the hammer to the pavement then and begins to dig. I see the little girl in the window reading a book with the sun shining onto her face. I see the black man with the rings fixing a rose to the lapel of his jacket. I see Francie smiling. Then there's a fierce hiss and a blaze and the air around Francie is shimmering in the heat. Flames pour out of his boots and his trousers and his shirt. His hair too is on fire. There is fire in his mouth. There is fire on his hands. His skin flames and then blackens. The jackhammer falls to the pavement and Francie along with it. Myles and John and Pat and the Iroquois and myself and the girl and the black man all look at him lying dead on the pavement beside the hole and the mains cable he cut through with the hammer, the insulation boiling and smoking and the coloured wires inside like the stems of cut flowers.

31

I look up and watch the ash form at the end of the cigarette balanced on the headboard. I watch the ash move and break up and fall onto the pillow beside me. Then I watch the fire in the cigarette burn into the wood. All along the headboard there are lines of cigarette burns like the black keys on a piano.

In Maggie's room way up at the top of the house in Elgin Avenue the headboard on her single bed had beading and vines and flowers engraved into it. The headboard was deep brown, the colour of stout. There was a small table covered with lace by the side of the bed and sometimes when we went into the bed together she would take the candle by the picture of the Sacred Heart and she would place it on this table so that we would have light. There was a way she looked in this light that gave me the sweetest peace. From the bed when she was sleeping I could look at the way she arranged the room. There was a shelf she had for books and a shelf for records and in between was a map of Ireland. The map not only told you where the cities and towns and rivers were but it also had little marks on it that told you about things that had happened. There was a mark that meant

ambush, a mark that meant battle, a mark that meant slaughter and a mark that meant the wasting of a town. The walls were white and the carpet was the colour of the grass that grows in sand. There was a picture of her cousin Eddie Furlong who was a champion fiddler from Monaghan town. There was a picture of her father down on one knee picking flowers for a child. There was a picture of me at Brighton Pier in the Tailor's suit that had worn so well with my hands in my pockets and with more hair than I have now. In this picture I am wearing Maggie's sunglasses. I loved the feeling of her breathing lightly on my neck when she was sleeping.

If she woke she did not fix her hair so that it would fall over the left eye. I could see the table with the mirror where she kept her bottles and scissors and combs that always had a different arrangement each time I was there. I could see the wardrobe which was sometimes open and when it was I could see the dress the colour of sand and all the other dresses and her hats and her blouses and her coats. I liked to see something out of place, like maybe the red leather shoe with the high heel tipped over onto its side. Things like this made me think of her doing things. The room was up at the top of the house just beneath the roof and the ceiling sloped down to either side of the bed and you felt enclosed and private like you were in a tent.

There was a window came out through the slope of the roof and I remember a tall glass there filled with irises. They were very still and blue in the first light of the Sunday morning after I'd played all night in a session for the landlord's wife's birthday in the Weaver's Arms. It was the month of May, the morning light a very pale blue. We had such hunger for each other all the way back home through the streets and up the stairs and into the bed where finally I could feel all the warmth and draw and power of her body. We drank brandy then in the bed, the sheets and the blankets rippled the way sand is under water, the pale blue light moving past the irises into the room. The air of the room seemed loaded with her as I breathed it in and I knew I had never felt so filled with the wonder of another person when she placed her lips up close to my ear and asked me to play for her. I see me now sitting up in the bed in my vest only, the bare white legs crossed, the hair on my head almost all gone too, moving a little from side to side with my accordion and with Maggie beside me with her hand resting on my knee and her red hair falling down on her white shoulders as I play for her very slow and sweet "My Lagan Love".

32

"Do you remember the way my hair was then? It was that long I had to move it to sit down. Do you remember the way Da begged me not to cut it?"

There are sixteen people in the upstairs room of the Eagle's Nest the day I marry Maggie and I did not think that Eileen would be among them. Mary that time was in a convent in Wales. Bernadette with her husband the publican in Belfast. They sent a telegram. Vincent last heard of was working with racehorses in Australia. I never found Joe, though I look still. Eileen I'd lost long ago too but Brid hadn't, even though she was away in Philadelphia with her six children and her husband who's a millionaire from building houses. Brid sent Eileen the message about the wedding. I would like to see Brid now. I remember the day a man from Galway Da knew from music competitions left a tin whistle down on a chair and Brid picked it up and could play even though she was only eight that time and never played before. She played "The Soldier's Song".

Eileen is laughing. When she laughs it sounds like someone is pressing on her throat. I cannot see the steps she took from Labasheeda to this room in Cricklewood on the day I was married. On her face there are many lines like the lines on maps which show rivers breaking up before they empty into the sea. Her hair is grey and there's a kind of orange in it like what would colour ice-cream. She is thin and when you look at her you think of the hardness of her bones. Her dress has white in it but is mostly orange the same colour as her hair. Her voice is thick now and the sound of Yorkshire where she lives moves through it the way the smell of leaves burning far away would flavour a breeze. She smokes cigarettes one after the other.

She speaks of her husband.

"I met him one day in a black fog going around a corner in the Holloway Road. The fog was so thick you could take a spoon to it. It was the first time I ever saw them use lanterns. It was like the frozen fogs they get in Russia where if you walk through them you leave the print of your body. I met him in a black fog and I never came out of it until the day he died. He was useless. He was worse than useless. Do you know I can upholster a settee? I can tell you the value of old clocks. I know about dress hats for women and the buying and selling of motor cars. I ran a hotel. I did these things because he didn't do a tap of work all his life and whatever I brought home he drank. I should have known better and stayed in out of the fog."

The laugh that sounds like there's a heavy liquid down in her lungs. I think looking at her that maybe she's not bitter but she's tough. Out on the floor they're doing a set. Eileen looks over and with the breeze of the dancers moving over her face and through her hair I can see as I look from the side at the arrangement of brow and nose and eyes something of what she was when she was a girl and nothing had disappointed her. The more she watches the dancers the more of what the years have put in her eyes lifts from her and goes.

"I was nursing when I first came over. I was in the Hackney Hospital. One time a man came in with terrible burns and the clothes were all stuck to his skin and they gave me the job of getting them off him and I collapsed right onto the floor before I even touched him. I knew I couldn't manage it then but before I quit it was St Patrick's Day and a crowd of us went in a coach to the Seymour Hall for a dance. We went to tea dances that time too at the Astoria. It cost sixpence. Everyone was beautifully turned out." She has her eyes still on the dancers.

"That time at the Seymour Hall I went out for a Paul Jones. We went around in our circles and when we stopped there was this man opposite me and of course we danced. He was in a black tie. He was absolutely immaculate. After the dance we sat down together. He told me he was a tea planter home from Assam. I can still see him. He was tall and dark, with horn-rimmed glasses. Very good looking. If he was to pass me on the street now I'd know him. We had two or three more dances together and then he asked me could he see me home. When I said this to the other girls they said it was too dangerous and I was to go back with them in the coach. But I went back with him anyway. He had a lovely car and I sat up beside him thinking of the life I might have on the tea plantation in Assam. He drove me right to the gate of the hospital, he shook hands with me and he said, 'Thank you for the lovely evening.' I've never forgotten him. He was a perfect gentleman. He had a lovely black coat with fur on the collar."

She stands up then and holds out her hand. I take it and we go out onto the floor. Martin is there with a big smile on him and the sweat pouring off his forehead. John

Conneely is standing ready with his wife, tapping his foot. Maggie finishes tying a bow in the hair of her niece and then turns to me. The look on her is like that of a valley just cleared of mist. The faces are red from the dance just ended, the skin shining, the chests rising and falling as they wait for the music to begin. They hold themselves like long-distance runners just before the start of a race. The meaning of a thing that brings you pleasure can come slowly but I got the fullness of this picture just when I saw it. Jack Dwyer puts his bow to the strings of his fiddle. Artie Sweeney's shoulders fly up as he squeezes his accordion. The man at the piano leans over and drops as he hits the note like a swimmer diving from a rock. The tune begins. Eileen is very light. Her bones could be made from the lightest wood. The music is like an electrical current driving us all around the floor. Eileen knows the steps without looking or thinking. The steps are inside her. She throws her head back and laughs and it's as though something in her face breaks and falls away, a mask made of dried clay. The way she spun me around at home the day of the Stations. Her feet now are like gulls as they dip and glide on the air. We pass the dancers, flashes of white and red from their clothes, breezes blowing. John Conneely charges through a gap with his wife, his bad knees springing him forward. The pulse of the music and the pulse of the dancers. We are all of us in the dance. The sound I heard from the kitchen at home as I waited by the door after I painted it green. Da lifting the accordion from its box and holding it out to Joe, his eyes shining. The way

he could blow into his flute and put the notes of "Anach Cuain" through you like stitches in a cloth. Joe Connor showing us the white stones of Donegal when he sang the day we killed the pig. Matt needing a tune like he would need a drop of spring water on a hot day. The accordion growing from my hands. The notes ringing in the iron hold of the boat to Liverpool. The way I found "She Moves Through the Fair" in the room with Francie in Kilburn. "My Lagan Love" for Maggie when she asked for it. Music happens inside you. It moves the things that are there from place to place. It can make them fly. It can bring you the past. It can bring you things that you do not know. It can bring you into the moment that is happening. It can bring you a cure.

33

The way Maggie was.

She could place a hat on her head at the perfect angle. She knew the names of trees. She could follow a tune or a notion or a story and see sense where others couldn't. She could weave. She could drink and never falter. She could mend wounds. She could speak so that it sounded like her voice was inside you. She could make a dress. She had knowledge of cities in Spain. She could win at any card game involving memory. She could fill an emptiness even when silent. She could swim great distances.

I remember the way she placed a handkerchief to her lips. I remember the way she held vegetables when cutting them, the way her hands moved, the fine bones and long fingers, everything light and slow and sure. She had a way when something amused her of moving her lips one way and her eye another. She was quick with sums. She took me to the museum to see the coloured birds of the Pacific. The sun could be hard on her, but only on her face. It made her look bothered and embarrassed. She couldn't stop her feet when she heard a tune. When sick she did not complain. When I asked her about the way she pushed up the two sides of her long red hair and let it fall so that it covered her left eye she held my hand very lightly and told me that the eye that was hidden was made of glass.

What was she like? She was not like an animal or a colour. She was not like the sky, or weather, or a kind of food or stone. She was like a forest. Things unknown to her lived and changed inside. The light never stopped moving. The age of the forest and its new growth. She could enclose you. Her silence. The wind could not touch you.

She was a woman. There was no part of her that was less, her step when turning a corner, her voice when close to you, her rings, her touch, her look when waking. I try to bring her here. Her rosary is here, her dress with the bluebells, the photographs. Her leg narrows in a long line from the knee. Her skin is the temperature of new bread. It glows a little like polished wood around her shoulders from her time in the sun. If she lifts her shoulders when explaining something the bones in her neck make hollows. The skin has a smell, of sun, of the bed and of lavender. Her laughter comes not from her throat but from within her centre. I see the sweep of her lines, the patterns in her skin, her movements. I follow them. I am enclosed within her. Then I cannot help myself. I see the sunlit street with the high plane trees with their bark the colour of ash, the motorcyclist roaring past, the dog moving out ahead of me. Maggie is in a crowd coming towards me. I see this again and again and again. She puts one hand on the top of her hat and waves with the other. The hand stalls, then drops.

34

When Dermot picks the field he will give us we begin to think of the caravan. We think of how it will look and where it will be placed. At the back of the field is a rockface of white stone streaked with grey. We will place the caravan here to keep it from the wind. Across the land as it slopes is the river where it breaks into the waterfall. The sun will rise over the back of the rockface and set over the river. Maggie talks of the gold light on the water at this time of day. There are blackberries along the stone wall that borders the lane and whitethorn, ash, wild cherry and sloe between the fields. Across the river are apple and pear trees in the orchard left behind by Lord Masborough. There are wild orchids there and you can see fish bones and the blue shells of crayfish left by otters. I am to put down potatoes and carrots and cabbage, and Maggie will look after the flowers and the mint.

If you follow the lane up over the hill behind the caravan you come to a turning. To the right you go down to the sea where Matt's nephew Hugh passes the days with lobster pots and winkles and dulse. To the left just a mile from the turning is Honor Casey's with its sides of bacon and rubber boots and pints. We can go there any evening we like for the work will be behind us. There are to be two rooms in the caravan. We're to have flowers through the summer and curtains bought in Belfast. We're to bring the bed made of oak

Maggie's mother slept in in Monaghan. We know the plates we will eat from, the glasses we will drink from and the pictures we will look at on the walls. We know how it will look through the bedroom window on a clear morning. We know how the whitethorn will look in May and the rowan berries in September. We know the smell and the light and the feeling of the air. When I was young I had no future and no past. After that I had work. I paved roads, I broke up concrete, I dug under houses and I shifted muck. I counted shovelfuls, I counted potatoes and I counted bricks. That was the time I got a past. The past was heavy, like the blocks used for ballast in a boat. Without a past I would have fallen. I thought I had a future too but I could not see it. It was in the things I lifted and carried and in what I was given for doing it. This was a future that flickered and darkened whenever I tried to look at it. Then without warning there was Maggie and there was light and there was a road ahead to receive us.

35

That Sunday evening as I walk out with the dog to meet Maggie the sun drops below the clouds and fills the street with light. The newspaper was on the table and a teacup beside it where she'd left them to go to Mass. When I get to the street with the high plane trees very thick that year with leaves I see from the people walking towards me that the Mass is over. People walk slowly after Mass. I hear from the park the sound of a tennis ball being struck. It is a beautiful evening in early August with the evening light a very rich gold shining on the white shirts and the dresses and in among them I can see Maggie in her hat walking towards me and the dog. I never in all the time I knew her could get used to the sight of her. There was always something in how she held her head or lifted her hand to arrange the trail of hair across her face, the bones in her hands, the sound she would make before laughing, the lines breaking around her mouth, her foot tapping lightly to a rhythm she was making in her mind, the graceful way she could bend or turn, the way she could listen like the words or the music were water falling over her, the way she could see into the root of what people did, how amazed she could be. Sometimes she would seem like a scientist the way she looked at how people were, the moves they made. These things about her were always new and they were always her. Nothing she did reminded me of anything I had seen before. How in all the world did I ever find her? She puts her hand on the top of her hat to hold it in the breeze and she waves. Her stride lengthens a little, and quickens. Then her hand stalls in the air, and drops. She looks like she has forgotten something. She moves to her right like she's going to fall, but she rights herself. She balances by the tips of her fingers on a low wall. Then twisting slowly in a long movement that seems to hold the whole of the day, her arms going out to the side while her head drops, she falls to the ground. I see her head bounce once on the paving stone. I see her hat twist and roll in the breeze down the street back towards the church as I run towards her.

I'll not be leaving Kentish Town now except in a brown box and when I do I'll be going to Labasheeda to lie with Maggie. I've left the instructions. The girl who lives in the flat downstairs knows what to do. The governor of the Gloucester Arms. The woman whose dog I walk on weekday afternoons. And I've written it all out on a paper that's on the table beside the bed. There's the key to the box that has the money. How many feet of tunnelling to buy a coffin? How many to send me to Labasheeda? These hands. Battered and scarred like all of our hands. What travels through the tunnels? Who drives over the roads? What happens within the brick walls? Do the people there think of the men who built them?

After the funeral in Monaghan I hire a taxi to take us to Labasheeda. I believe the soil here is only an inch deep and after that it's blue clay. There's hills rolling and the sound of rushing water as everywhere in Ireland. I look at a hill and I see Maggie rushing down it on the back of a horse as a young girl and it's like I've touched a raw wire. What is there to think of but her? Over everything I see there is the colour of her death.

Across the border and along it as we drive, set among the hills just like those hills of Monaghan, are the high towers of the English with their guns and helicopters and electrical instruments. There are fires burning too in the hills, bonfires. I think of the fires we built at Hallowe'en to drive away the spirits that fly. The roads here leading over the border end in heaps of concrete where they were blown up by the soldiers that live in the towers.

What is it to miss someone? It is not the throbbing ache of a wound. It is not the pain you get under your ribs from running. It is not a befouled feeling, the feeling of being in mud. It is the feeling of being in a strange place and losing direction. It is the feeling of looking without seeing and eating without tasting. It is forgetfulness, the inability to move, the inability to connect. It is a sentence you must serve and if the person you miss is dead your sentence is long.

I stand where the road rises over Labasheeda after burying Maggie in the graveyard. I hear again the black earth falling over her coffin. Then the silence. There is no comfort

or no ending of anything with the earth settling over her where she rests but there is pity and there is peace, or maybe a picture of a peace that will be one day. The sky is black and deep blue and very still. I see all the grains in the paving of the road, the yellow-painted stripes where once there were tracks of gravel and dirt. The yellow is glowing. There is thistle blooming purple by the side. I begin to walk. The cries of birds sound against the low sky. I pass the house of Philly Concannon who was a good footballer, the green iron gate rusted now and faded from sunlight and rain, bindweed stitched through the gaps and the path where they walked no longer to be seen for it's grown over now with high grass. My walk is strange as I go along the road, slow and halting like I've stones in my shoe. I can hear the river. It is softer now than it was for the banks too like the paths are thick with grass. On the hillside by Knocksouna there are sheep, a man walking towards them slowly with his dog. There are cows. I can see three and I hear another in a field below. But the animals are few. Fields wet and covered with rushes, the walls falling. This is the time of day when once it seemed I knew where everyone was. I pass the pump, the concrete around it stained with rust, the handle dangling like a broken arm. I walk on towards the bend in the road. The silence is very heavy with only the birds calling as they pass. Away on the ridge by the path that leads down to Killycolpy I can see three houses. They are shells, black shells now at the end of the day with the dim light going. Here then were Brennans, Murtaghs and Dolans. Everyone gone now. I lean over onto a wall by the side of the road and light a cigarette. A car passes behind me, taking the bend slowly. I watch after it. It passes the Tailor's house, the roof gone there too, grass growing up from the kitchen floor around the legs of a table standing alone. It passes Dermot's house, the little house he built in the field where Ma kept the hens and then painted pink. His car is parked in the drive. There's a big tin saucer beside it for receiving television signals. The car that passed behind me winds past the houses and stops in the road before the three houses standing on the ridge. I see a man step out from the back seat and hand money to the driver. He walks

up the path towards the houses. I stand away then from the wall and begin to move after him. I hear small stones break beneath my feet. I hear myself breathing. As I pass I look in through the window of Matt's and see that the kitchen is filled with potatoes, eggcups full of nails and Matt's pipe still sitting on the ledge. I stop in the road and turn to look at the house where I was born. The door is blue now, hanging by a hinge. If I could draw music from the air I would place it behind the door. I would fill the rooms with people. I would look into their faces and listen to their speech. But I cannot find them. They are passing. There is only the sound of the river drifting through grass, the wind rising. There is the smell of wet ash and wet wood. On the ridge beyond I see the man moving around the forsaken houses. He is wearing a brown suit that is too small for him and he drags his right leg. Again I begin to walk. The names of the places around me begin to weaken and fade. The car where Tom Connor kept his pigs is still in the yard, rusted to its axles. At the lane leading to the long field I meet Baby. She has a new pram, high wheels and the chrome gleaming. "You're still here, Baby," I say. "If I wasn't here who would there be to leave footprints?" she says. We walk along together. We are heading without reason to where the man is moving around the houses on the ridge. The wind picks up a little more and Baby feels it might rain. "The cruel wind of the north," she says. When we get to the spot where the man got out of the taxi we stop. We watch through the gaps in the walls as he moves through the middle house. "Do you know him?" I say to Baby. "I do," she says. "Tommy Murtagh. Went to England long ago and cuts

grass in the parks." He comes out then from behind the house and moves down through the yard. He stumbles over the wet stones. When he gets to a tree he stops. The tree is low, the branches black and tormented looking from being lashed in the wind. He kneels down then in the long grass before the tree and he folds his hands. "Comes back once a year and haunts the house," says Baby. "Haunts the tree too." She smells of leather and soap. Lower, blacker clouds roll in from the north and with them comes the rain. I lift the jacket up over my head and watch the man as he looks down at the roots of the tree, the rain pouring over him. Birds

scream in the sky and the man looks up. It is as though he has not heard this sound before, as though he does not know where he is. I get the smell of leather and soap again and Baby's face is before me. "Would you know now what's under the tree?" she says. Her face is fallen in around the mouth where the teeth have gone. She looks like she might laugh. "I don't," I say. "Tommy Murtagh's twin brother. Born dead and never baptised. So they buried him under the tree." She nods once at the strangeness of this knowledge. I look past her to the man. He's up now and looking around. He turns his collar up and he goes out onto the road.

In the rain the land seems to let go of what it carries. Who now can there be to know what the fish does in the well, where Joe Roddy took his heart attack, how much sand Matt hauled up on his donkey to build the field? Who will know the stories of who lies beneath the stones in the grave-yard? I walk now with nothing along with me, no sounds, no pictures, nothing of what was in happiness or in pain. I walk in forgetfulness, all that I pass seeming to vanish as I go.

36

In the room now a breeze comes in through the window and on it there is the smell of spring. Downstairs the girl turns on her radio. I lie in the bed and listen to its music. There is a time after long work when you can look for strength and there is nothing there. This is a time of forgetfulness and after comes a time when you know again what you can do. There can be a time too when the work is complete.

In the morning light I let go.

Acknowledgements

Many Irish emigrants were generous with their time and their stories. These include Willie Barratt, Ann Connolly, James Dunleavy, Dermot Grogan, Mary Hall, Martin Hayes, Evelyn Haynes, Maureen Heston, Joseph Hynes, Gerry McLaughlin, Peggy Moore, J. M. O'Neill, Tim O'Sullivan, Jessie Stafford, Michael Sullivan, Peter Woods and residents and staff at Arlington House. Peter Woods also granted permission to reprint his poem. Others who, in different ways, provided help include John Adamson, Jackie and Campbell Bruce, Zelda Cheatle, the Clifford family, Willie Collins, Hannah Dawes and Gary McKeone of the Arts Council, Seamus Deane, Catherine Eccles, the Faherty family, Vince Goodsell, Chris Jones, Declan Kiberd, Phillip Kirwin, Dewi Lewis, Gordon MacDonald, Christy McNamara, Metro Imaging, Michael Mitchell, Chrissie Redmond, Mark Sealy, Sarah Westcott, Jonathan Worth, and the people at the Harvill Press. Dermot Healy was an inspiration. John Berger fathered this book through his collaborations with Jean Mohr and his writing about migrant labourers. He read it and advised about its presentation, as well as writing the preface. Nichola Bruce collaborated valuably in finding the connections between the pictures and the words.

Many others not named here, including the subjects of the photographs, have been helpful in the production of this book, and the authors would like to express their gratitude to them also.

Picture Information